LAUREL

SALLY SAVIC

ELYSIAN FIELDS

"A REWARDING READ . . . AS A LOVE STORY, AS A WORK OF RICH, DESCRIPTIVE FICTION, AND AS AN ATMOSPHERIC PIECE ABOUT NEW ORLEANS."
—*The Chattanooga Times*

"Sally Savic's first novel puts her in the ranks of greatness." —*Star-News* (Pasadena)

"Rich in its implications about how we wrestle with good and evil, the ideal and the real, *ELYSIAN FIELDS* is for Sally Savic a striking debut as an author of quality contemporary literature."
—*Columbus Sunday Dispatch*

"An evocative and haunting tale. . . . Savic writes the kind of prose that makes poets jealous."
—*The Orlando Sentinel*

"Brilliantly crafted. . . . Savic uses the southern setting masterfully. . . . Her images breathe awfulness and rivet the reader's attention like a traffic accident."
—*The West Coast Review of Books*

"Sally Savic has a knack for describing emotional, as well as sexual, situations. . . . Her passages are alive with human dimension."
—*The Commercial Appeal* (Memphis)

"[Sally Savic] examines the nature of love, loss, and the inability of people to possess each other. The texture of New Orleans—its sound, its odor, its taste—is deftly reproduced." —*Library Journal*

Elysian Fields

A NOVEL

SALLY SAVIC

A LAUREL TRADE PAPERBACK
Published by
Dell Publishing
a division of
Bantam Doubleday Dell Publishing Group, Inc.
666 Fifth Avenue
New York, New York 10103

ISBN: 0-440-50182-2

Reprinted by arrangement with Charles Scribner's Sons

Printed in the United States of America
Published simultaneously in Canada

December 1989

10 9 8 7 6 5 4 3 2 1

W

For Lew and my parents

I am grateful to the Ohio Arts Council
for their support while writing this book;
and to Janet for her love and encouragement.

Elysian Fields

One

I found a photograph of Marshall inside one of his shoes in the closet. His good shoes, oxfords as solid as tree trunks, bought for fifty cents at a garage sale last summer. The picture was tucked up into the toe, and I don't know why it occurred to me to stick my hand into his shoe, but I'm always looking for clues about Marshall.

The picture was taken in 1967 when Marshall was fifteen. He's standing on the slippery bank of a murky, yellow bayou, and behind him the truncated trees dip into the still water. His eyes are like two green cat's-eye marbles filled with light. It's raining and his hair, the color of Georgia clay, lies slick against his pale skull like a helmet. He's smiling slightly at the camera. There's something brave about that smile—the audacious smart of being fifteen, ineffable, impudent, all-seeing, and unknowing. I held the picture for a long time. I caught sight of my own face, a dusty reflection in the dresser mirror and I thought, *He's more beautiful than me, I believe in his face more than mine.* . . .

Marshall's mother, Lucy Nell, says Marshall looks just like his father, but I saw a picture of his father once, a big stooped fellow with protruding dark eyes, a red, slip-sliding mouth, a sloppy nose. Nothing Like Marshall's bold bones, wide, slim mouth, pale eyes.

Lucy Nell slapped me when I said so. "You ain't the right girl," she said in her Arkansas twang. Her voice sounds like a guitar string when it busts, and sometimes it still zings through the room long after she's gone.

Lucy Nell stops by the house once or twice a week to take back the presents she gave us when Marshall and I were first married: a wrought iron planter, a crippled and dented barbecue grill, a wooden cross with a corn-husk Jesus she nailed to our front door. One afternoon I came home from work to find her ripping out seven yards of chicken wire she'd given us for the garden. When she came to take back her washing machine, she laid her head down on it and cried. "He's dead," she wailed, grazing her knuckles against the rinse cycle button. No one had ever said this out loud before.

The rinse cycle bumped on and water began streaming into the barrel of the washing machine. I started to bawl right alongside Lucy Nell there in the laundry room. When she saw me, she took my wrist in her bony hands and twisted it.

"Stop that, missy, or I'm gonna think you're to blame."

After she'd gone, I went through his drawers again, searched his pockets, counted the change he'd dropped months ago on top of the dresser, plucked a single strand of his hair from a dirty plastic comb in the bathroom. But I found nothing new, nothing telling. No letters, no ticket stubs, no mysterious receipts from motels or dry cleaners or pawn shops, no notes to himself. Just a hazy

photo of a boy on the banks of a bayou, a boy more
beautiful than me.

When Marshall first disappeared, we didn't even think
or bother to call the police. This was Marshall. Marshall
knew about the world. No one could touch him unless he
let them. But I had never thought of him dead. I always
tried to imagine other things. Marshall turning on the
Magic Fingers machines in tacky motel rooms. Marshall
catching trains and slow boats to sad, forgotten places,
pinpointing destinations on maps no longer current, bumping through the darkness of a world that no longer goes by
the same names. Siam. Atlantis. Babylon. And sometimes,
I thought of him living the glamorous life, jumping in
and out of automobiles named after jungle animals, dime-
dancing the nights away in dim, jazzy clubs, miles and
miles away from this town. But dead? No. Not Marshall.

I think Marshall was having an affair. With Corinthia.
Corinthia Jones. I looked her name up in the phone book
to make sure she was real. I called the number to hear her
voice. Corinthia sang in a Cajun band and dragged a sickly
child around by the wrist wherever she went. That was the
last time I saw Marshall. The night of Corinthia. Someone
was having a party and she was standing in the kitchen,
rinsing glasses, her eyes a splash of violet light, her nose
flat as an anvil. She turned to look at us when we came in,
and she and Marshall stared at one another as though there
was no one else in the world. Her kid began to cry as she
and Marshall followed each other through the rooms of the

house, furtive, yet always surprised, as though they'd bumped into one another on a street corner, their desire mere coincidence.

I looked down at the child. His eyes wet, his hair cropped short and fine as the silken tassel on an ear of corn, he bared his tiny teeth at me as if he knew I was as impotent as he and despised me for it.

Corinthia's red dress seemed to be calling Marshall. It shimmered in the kitchen's yellow light. Later, he followed her out to the grape arbor in the backyard. He held a cat high above her head and she laughed, her voice fluttering like wind chimes. But he's my husband, *my husband,* I thought, watching them there. He put the cat on her head and bent to kiss her on the mouth. The cat screamed and leaped into the lilacs. His mouth was still there. I could see his mouth more clearly than I'd ever seen it before. I could feel it on my own mouth. I could feel the soft fullness of it pressing, pressing until it suffocated me.

"Don't," I said as he reached for her waist.

Later I heard him unlocking the front door, the metal click, the silent shuffle upstairs. When he came inside the room, the lights from passing cars bobbed and spun around the walls and ceiling, and for one brief second, his face rose out of the blackness and he was looking into his future. I saw strangers in his eyes, places I'd never been, a life beyond me. In the crook of his arm was a jack-o'-lantern, its toothless grin caving in. He placed it gently on the bed beside my foot, patting it, twisting its stem hat into place.

He'd spent the long walk home making up a story. An

especially good one. A story worthy of belief. But I couldn't listen to another story. He was too good at it. I was bone tired of the truth lying to me as open and harsh as a slap across the face. He believed history would make sense of this if we could wait that long. But I couldn't wait. I watched the shadows on the wall, his fist dark and enormous coming toward me. The window behind us rattled with the deafening flap of blackbirds beating their wings against the panes. I could feel his warm breath, the words formed and unspoken against my face as he leaned closer, his hand cramped in threat. I closed my eyes, waiting for the heaviest of weights to reach me. I heard it hit with a wet, pulpy thwack. But it wasn't my face. It was the jack-o'-lantern's, its open jaw surprised. He fell heavily against the bed, pinning me down. But when I opened my eyes, it was the pumpkin staring at me, damp and cold on my chest. I pushed it to the floor, but I could still feel its weight pinning me against myself.

It's quiet tonight. From inside, through an open window, I can hear a radio talk show on the transistor in the kitchen. Mrs. Adele Corners from Happy Jack, Louisiana, is asking how to get a porkchop bone out of the porcelain canal of her toilet.

"How did the porkchop bone get there, Mrs. Corners?" the talk show host wants to know. His voice is round and smooth and full of insinuation.

"Somebody threw it down there," Mrs. Corners says breathlessly.

Rain is moving in from across the gulf, gathering its own blue darkness and thunder. The air is heavy with the sweet, clean smell of melon rinds. Inside the trees, the birds are making a big noise, settling down for the night, their black silhouettes teetering on the limbs of the large oak in the front yard. From the porch swing, I gaze through the picture window, pretending this is someone else's house, looking with a stranger's eyes. It's an old lady's house. A nest of comfort and finicky tastes. I've never moved the furniture, never added anything of my own to the confusion of antiques and musty draperies and rugs. My step-grandmother's house.

Violette Mattigan Marie Robichaux. She married my grandfather in 1964 in Kansas City while on a motoring tour of the West with her sister. My grandfather was in Kansas City on business, studying methods of preserving pork and beef. He had his own meat packing plant in Ohio.

I was ten when he brought Violette to Ohio. She was never considered family by my mother and my mother's brother and sister. No one treated her like she belonged to us. Not even my grandfather, who often stared at her as though she was something he could not quite believe in. Like a story he had read as a boy that he loved to read again and again but never considered possible. An immigrant from Hungary, he made his money slinging great hunks of meat, slabs of cow and pig, breaking bones, chopping and slicing and making flesh edible. There were stains on his clothing, even his best suits speckled, his white shirt cuffs edged brown with old blood. And Violette was a southern belle, an aging debutante, a woman too refined to wash her own dishes or work a garden. For a long time, I didn't believe she went to the bathroom like everybody else. I waited in the hall outside the door to hear the toilet flush.

No, my grandfather didn't really know Violette. He couldn't talk to her; their vocabularies were as alien as foreign languages. He had no idea how to love her. Only me. Only I loved her. I loved her the way you love memories not really your own but born into you, like lives you lived while your real self slept unaware. I wanted something from her, my small heart bursting to hold it, to take it from her, though I couldn't say what it was. I couldn't stand before the window of a store and point to it, name it. I wanted those green nights beneath drooping willows. I wanted to drink the magnolia's scent, make it mine. I wanted to hold the air about her in my hands, crawl beneath her skin and wear her on my own small, unready body. I wanted to be her.

But Violette wasn't long for our world. Grandfather sent her back to New Orleans when I was fourteen. She had learned to hate Ohio, had grown too old, too sad and faded in its unfriendly light. He took her down to the train one Sunday afternoon and was back the following Sunday. He bought her a small house on Prytania Street, and once a year, out of a sense of honor, he took the Delta Queen from Cincinnati to visit her. When she died, alone in her house with her maid Cleva Pear, I was twenty. When I was twenty-one, the house was mine. I came right away, as though I'd been summoned, my skin humming and unwilling to be touched as my family tried to keep me from leaving. And the time it took to get here, to New Orleans, to this life calling for me, seemed unbearable. What did I hope to find here?

Violette's dreams empty now and waiting to be claimed?
Or maybe Marshall.

Across the street, Mrs. Hooter comes out of her front
porch with a broom and shouts at a couple of dogs ripping
apart a trash bag at the bottom of her yard. The dogs look
up and sniff the air. One is yellow with a sharp, insolent
nose. The other's white coat is gray with dust. Mrs.
Hooter comes down into the yard and tries to hit them
with the broom. She bats at their tails, and they go loping
off into the twilight like a pair of gazelles. Down the
street, Penny, my next-door neighbor, is walking home
from the streetcar stop, her high heels clacking angrily
against the pavement. She's very fat. The light behind her
illuminates the blonde nylon wig perched on her head like
a flustered bird.

"Hey, Alice, what you doin tonight?"

"Why don't you come up?" I ask. I wait to meet
her at the gate and lead her into the green shadows
beneath the trees. I never knew anyone like Penny in
Ohio. I'm sometimes in love with her voice, her clothes
and shoes, her wigs, her fatness. As she totters beside me,
her high heels sink into the damp mud.

"I'm gonna break my leg," she frets.

The porch swing is old, and worm-eaten wood groans
crankily under her weight. She arranges an armful of
shopping bags at her feet.

"Look at this," she says, pulling a scarf from one of
the sacks. The scarf is cheap, polyester, with a flower pot
hand-painted on its fluorescent yellow surface. It's so ugly
it makes me sad.

"That's nice."

"Only cost fifty-nine cents at the Woolworth side-walk sale," she says. She ties the scarf under her neck, squashing the synthetic curls. A pale Aunt Jemina.

"A bargain."

"Sure," she says, "and I got a pretty little Maybelline compact for ten cents, too." She takes a chocolate moonpie out of her purse and tears the plastic wrapper off with her teeth. "You got some beer, dontcha?"

I go into the kitchen and bring back six cold bottles that begin to sweat the second I take them from the refrigerator.

"Lucy Nell was lurkin round here today while you was at work," Penny tattles between chews. She wrestles the cap off the beer bottle with the hem of her muumuu. Lucy Nell and Penny are archenemies. Sometimes when Lucy Nell comes over, she stands at the hedge between Penny's yard and mine and glares at Penny's house, willing Penny to come outside so she can pick a fight.

"She says to me, 'Miz Lapere, if yore yard don't look like a junkpile, I don't know what a junkpile is.' I told her to mind her own bizness, and she starts hollerin bout some citizens committee she's gonna call. She don't even live in this neighborhood."

"Don't pay attention to her."

Penny frowns at the empty moonpie wrapper and digs through her purse for another one.

"If you let that harpy in yore front door, she's gonna make off like a bandit with everything you own," Penny counsels. Moonpie crumbs are stuck to her lipsticked mouth. She tosses Kleenex and candy bar wrappers from her purse onto her lap.

"Did Boy take my last pie?" she cries. "He's always in my purse!"

Boy is Penny's son. He's a vagrant, a hoodlum, a ne'er-do-well, unemployed since he got out of high school six years ago. When Marshall first moved in with me, he and Boy would sit on the porch all day drinking beer and watching cars go by. Sometimes they'd count out-of-state license plates, and Marshall would give me the tally when I got home from work. Five from Utah. Three from New Mexico. Boy is younger than Marshall, but they went to the same school, lived in the same neighborhood, hung out with the same friends. Sometimes Marshall had a job. He subbed at a bar in the French Quarter for an old lady named Miss Hilda who had a wooden leg and a German accent. Miss Hilda played the piano. When she was sick, Marshall filled in for her. But the customers didn't like Marshall as much as Miss Hilda. He was a better piano player, but he had no enthusiasm and he refused to sing along with the show tunes. Certain songs he wouldn't play even if the management threatened him: "Moon River," anything from *Mary Poppins* or *Fiddler on the Roof,* and that trombone song from *The Music Man.* But Miss Hilda liked Marshall and always called him when she needed a replacement.

Marshall played the piano by ear. He'd never had lessons and didn't know how to read music. If he'd heard a song before, he could play it. This was a gift from God, Lucy Nell claimed. She had plans for Marshall's career. She saw him in a pale blue tuxedo, playing in the bar at the Fairmont Hotel. She bought a plastic Christmas candelabra and urged Marshall to set it on the piano when he played. She still talks about Marshall's piano career, even though he's gone. She accuses me of poisoning Marshall's mind against the piano, of making him feel foolish about it. She read in the obituaries that Miss Hilda had died, and for a week, she was frantic to find Marshall, to bring him back home so he could fill that empty piano bench. She still keeps her high hopes intact. Like Penny's high hopes for Boy, whose joblessness has become a way of life. Penny, like Lucy Nell, dreams up careers for Boy, imagines him swinging onto the streetcar in a three-piece suit and patent leather shoes. She comes home with pamphlets from the Marine Corps and the Army. She reads the want ads every day, imagining Boy as a bank manager, a car salesman, an advertising executive. Once I suggested that he get a modest job, employment as a cashier or a pizza delivery boy. But this offended Penny. She told me Boy had been born with a veil over his face and that the nurses at Charity Hospital had promised her that his life would be prosperous, lucky, filled with good fortune.

"I spect he ain't found his callin yet," she told me, smiling brightly, whisking hopelessness back under the rug.

Penny gulps down the last two inches from a bottle of beer and reaches for another one. The magnolia rustles against the screens around the porch, the scent wafting through the air.

"How's work, Alice?" Penny pipes, digging through her purse for an emery board. Once I overheard Penny telling Mrs. Hooter that I was the editor of the *Times Picayune*, though Mrs. Hooter knew better and brought out her edition of the paper to prove it. I work for a trade paper called *The Lagniappe,* typing classifieds, but Penny still likes to think I run *The Picayune* single-handedly no matter how many times I tell her it isn't so.

Out on the street, a car door slams and a horn honks the first few bars of "Dixie." A dog barks fiercely, hoarsely on somebody's front porch.

"That's Boy, I bet," Penny says. "His friend Lumey bought that car horn in Alabama last week."

We can hear Boy flailing at the bushes between our houses, his tennis shoes squeaking.

"Over here, Boy," Penny calls.

He blunders against the screen behind me, his face appearing like magic above the railing. Boy doesn't talk to me. He's never said a word to me unless Marshall was there to hear it too.

"Mama," he says, "gimme ten dollars."

"Boy," she whines and grabs her purse to her bosom. Boy stares at the purse, his nose pressed flat against the screen. His eyes are big, the pupils black and starry.

"Mama," he says, suddenly bored, his lids droopy. He yawns so wide I can look into the cavern of his mouth and count his long, pale teeth.

"I don't have no money," Penny complains. "Them hospital bills are comin in every day. How'm I supposed to keep you in whiskey and short pants at the same time?"

"Lumey's waiting," he offers. He lights a cigarette and leans into the screen, considering me. The cigarette dangles from his lip, and despite myself, I'm impressed. This is a fellow who knows how to smoke a cigarette. He squints one eye against the column of smoke rising toward it. We stare at each other. I want to look away, but I can't. There's something pretty and smooth about his face;

he has his mother's skin and an aura of plumpness, though he's reedy, almost gaunt. He winks at me and smiles, his lips dry and smooth like a polished stone, thin and knife-sharp.

"I only got five," Penny says, counting out a handful of crumpled ones.

"Mama . . ." His breath is heavy against the back of my neck and smells sweetly of marijuana. Penny rustles through the pockets of her muumuu, pulling out used Kleenex. She finds an extra five-dollar bill and hands it to me with the ones. I hold the money in my hand; I don't want to give it to him.

"There's a hole here, Alice," he says, poking a long finger through an opening in the screen. It's the first time I've heard him say my name. I shove the wad of money through the hole and he snatches it, like a frog licking a fly from the air. He laughs. I feel a strange sense of loss as though this has happened to me before.

"Get home early," Penny says. Boy counts the money and stuffs it into the pocket of his jeans. He nods at Penny and turns, pushing rhododendron branches out of his way. After a moment, we hear the car door slam and Lumey plays the Dixie horn again.

"All them hospital bills," Penny laments.

Last fall, Penny took the bus downtown and as she was getting off, the driver shut the door on her leg and drove away. He dragged her about half a block until someone in the back of the bus heard her screaming and asked the driver to stop. The bus driver took off his shiny sunglasses and looked down at her.

"You in a heap of trouble, lady," he said, looming over her, waiting for the ambulance to come.

The transit company claims the accident was the result of personal negligence and won't cover Penny's hospital bills. A few nights back, Penny and I were in Gino's Lounge and she got this idea that we should sneak over to the bus barn on Oak Street and slash all the bus tires. Gino was behind the bar, wearing a knitted hat with Budweiser cans stapled to the brim.

"Today I bought me a watch," he complained, "from a nigger in a panama hat on Canal Street, and already it don't work."

Gino used to be a Merchant Marine. He has empty liquor bottles from all over the world behind the bar, lit up like trophies. Every two months or so, when the moon is full, he bangs on his jukebox and hides about fifty dollars worth of quarters so he can collect the insurance. Everybody knows he does it; nobody blames him.

Gino loaned Penny the paring knife he used for slicing lemons.

"If they put you gals in Central Lockup," he said, "don't be tellin em where you got the knife."

We took the streetcar down to Oak Street. The barn was lit with fluorescent lights, full of grimy buses parked side by side in long rows. A bald man sat in the back office, his feet propped up on a file cabinet, snoring beneath a magazine. We snuck down a row out of his sight and knelt before the front tire of one of the buses. The tire was too thick, the paring knife too flimsy. I sat on my haunches and watched Penny carve. I smoked a cigarette and looked at her sad, chubby face, her hennaed red hair lying flat and limp against her round head. I saw how much more cheerful she was in a wig. I felt a great swelling in my heart. False hope pedaled up like an errand boy with a message of good will. I wanted to change Penny's life, reroute history, make her a beauty.

Then I stood up to stretch my legs. I ground out the cigarette with the toe of my sneaker and remembered what we were doing. Penny was sweating. She was breathing hard, and when she turned her face to me, I could see she wasn't drunk any more. Her face puckered up and went pale.

"I cain't do it," she puffed. "I'm too good." She burst into tears. I took her arm and helped her to her feet.

"I'm just too good," she cried.

There are four beers left in the refrigerator. The radio is playing a version of "I Left My Heart in San Francisco" by a singing parrot. The parrot's voice is frightfully human, like the sorry bray of a drunk.

"Who's that singin in there?" Penny calls. "It ain't Tony Bennett."

I bring the rest of the beer to the porch and sit down across from her. She wipes a mustache of perspiration from her upper lip with the back of her chubby arm.

"I got to get me some money," Penny says. She stares through me, past me. Penny believes there are ways to get-rich-quick. Once she told me it was un-American for me to think any differently.

"We could sell drugs," she murmurs, her voice and eyes still far away.

"I'm not selling drugs."

"Boy says you can make a lot of money selling drugs,

and you don't have to pay taxes. I could buy me a Persian rug."

"What do you want with a Persian rug?"

"Boy's got a friend who sells drugs, and he's got a Persian rug and a fourteen-inch color TV set. I sure would like to have me a color set."

"You gotta be kidding. They'd put you in jail."

"That's what I told Boy," she says quickly. "I told him it was against the law."

"That's right."

"He says if yore careful, you don't get caught. He says maybe somebody down at Gino's Lounge would buy some from us."

"Penny, the people at Gino's Lounge are your friends. Do any of them take drugs?" There's almost nobody that haunts Gino's that isn't over forty-five except me, and I only go with Penny. These people drink highballs for excitement. Penny thinks about it for a moment and shakes her head sadly.

"Umm," she considers. "I was just thinkin, Alice, that's all."

"Enter a sweepstakes. Play bingo down at the church on the corner. I hear you can win fifty bucks if you get your card filled."

I try to imagine Penny as a drug dealer. Meeting potential buyers at the door in her muumuu and feathered house slippers. Haggling over the price of an ounce. It makes me mad to think of strangers in Penny's house, the kind of strangers Marshall brought home with him from bars late at night, people with tattoos, and nicknames like Mambo and Bubba. Marshall loved people with nicknames. He admired tattoos, though he didn't have one himself.

I look up at her and hand her another beer. We drink together, the beer hitting the back of our throats with a dry, airy crack. Penny kicks off her high heels. Her bare feet, the nails pink with polish, are strangely slim and juvenile, like a young girl's, the tiny nails like pearls.

"Mayo asked me to a party Saturday night," she says. "Out at the Pontchartrain Beach Amusement Park. He's got tickets to go on all the rides for free."

"I thought Mayo was married."

"He is. But he's gonna divorce himself."

"That's good." I don't know why I believe Mayo will leave his wife and three kids for Penny, but I do. Maybe it's just for tonight I believe it. The rain has finally come and it sprinkles down the canvas awning. The night is deep with secrets and possibilities. I think of Boy, the shadows of his face, the way that cigarette hung from his mouth with the ash lengthening until I thought it would fall, but it didn't. His gaze was so steady, his slim lips so perfectly pursed around the butt. I feel a sudden trill of fear along my spine, a hunger for something secret and dark.

"Mayo's got hair on his elbows," Penny confides, yawning wide, the inside of her mouth pink like a baby's.

"Well, that's okay."

"I never seen it on nobody else. I told him to shave it off."

The thought of Mayo shaving the hair off his elbows makes me sad.

"It don't look right," Penny chatters.

"Don't make him do that," I say, stifling a sleepy burp. When Mayo and Penny rendezvous, he always brings her a present: a ring from Yellowstone Park, a plastic daffodil, a package of Little Debbie cupcakes. He's always laughing, never speaks below a holler. Even if he doesn't divorce himself for Penny, he's a lucky charm, a good sign, a sturdy wooden cross to hold up against demons.

"Mayo's a wonderful guy," I hear myself saying, my voice small and faraway. I feel relieved when I think of Marshall. For the first time, I feel sorry for him and not me. I'm no longer privy to all that sadness he carried around with him. I don't have to understand him for this one moment in front of me. I don't have to love him or miss him. For a single moment in time, I'm free.

Still, it would be good to see his face. It would be good to make things right. And in this moment, I believe I could. I believe I could right the wrongs, turn the tables, make him look at me and love me and never want to leave me.

"Penny, have another beer," I say. But I'm thinking, Penny, help me keep this night from turning, keep the stars hanging tight and in place, the rain dripping from the leaves . . . I want to feel this certain at least until tomorrow.

"Penny," I whisper, leaning toward her. But she's sleeping. Her head tucked into her soft bosom, her slim, delicate feet sticking straight out, her body abandoned. Her legs are parted and when the wind carries a light breeze across the porch, her muumuu rises and I can see her underpants, a startling fuchsia. Penny, my friend. We can call down hope from the darkest sky.

Two

The monotonous hum of the typewriters echoes against the blank walls. I hold my hands high and rounded the way Mrs. Almond taught me to play the piano when I was nine. The ceiling fan makes lopsided swoops above my head and it's so hot and close in this office, the collar of my blouse is damp with sweat. These are the dog days. Marshall told me about the dog days, pointing out the Dog Star, the dippers, the Seven Sisters.

I think of Marshall as a boy lying in a sleeping bag in the backyard, naming the stars, catching moths and lazy flies in a bug jar. Marshall's childhood seems more real to me than my own. Those sweaty nights out back, that boy in his underwear snatching fireflies, listening to the cicadas and the racket his parents made in the kitchen. Always ready for escape, like a hobo, with his baggage in his pockets, always with his hand on the door to slip away from his father's hammy, restless hands, his mother's eager, smothering love.

Marshall is boyish still, clever like an urchin. He knows the flimflam man's tricks, the pickpocket's smooth moves. He doesn't care if he is penniless, destitute, homeless; he only expects to survive. And sometimes it seems to me that he's not of this world. A fallen angel too far from home to turn back but willing to take what the earth has left to offer. A shining core lights him from inside out, makes him more vivid than other people and more mercurial, too hot or too cold.

I've studied his habits and still there are many things I've never seen Marshall do, many things I'll never know. I've never seen him wear a suit, never seen him read a book or even the newspaper, though he brings the paper home every day. I've never seen him sick or helpless. He's never cried in front of me. He bites his fingernails but I have never seen him do it.

I miss his habits. His boots at the bottom of the stairs to trip over in the dark. His clothes in a heap on the floor by the bed so if something happened, a fire or an emergency, he could jump into them quickly. His sleeping like the dead, standing up, sitting down, or on the floor. Marshall could take off and put on his drunkenness like a hat. He knew about building things like chicken coops, cabinets, tree houses. He could speak a little Cajun French, and when he played the piano he could make you forget where you were, though he always looked uncertain, confused, even a little frightened, as if he were playing for the first time and wasn't sure of the notes. When Marshall went out at night to drink with his friends, he always brought me something: a pickled egg, a Hav-a-Hank, a Blind Robin, maybe a small bag of corn chips.

He is best at love. He loves a body, Marshall does. A woman's body. He has true reverence, a holy approach. I flush to think of it, from my toes to my nose, blood blooming. Marshall, his face quiet above mine, his eyes wide open. Even now, months and months away from Marshall, I fidget in this hard plastic chair thinking of it. Ashamed, perhaps, sometimes prideful, too. But mostly filled with fear. The kind of fear you feel watching a fight, drunken men slamming each other's heads against car hoods, pummeling, planting fists against flesh. It is a strange fear, a beckoning hand. You can't turn away from it but you can't reach out to stop it. It touches you either way.

Looking up, I see my reflection in the dirty window. My cheeks burn, and I turn back to my typewriter and peck: CHOW CHOW PUPS FOR SALE BY OWNER. And, MORT WISHES A HAPPY WEDDING DAY TO HIS X FIANCEE JEZEBEL. I think of Marshall all the time.

Gypsy and Lorraine, the other girls in the office, are arguing about how to spell "gourmet." The late afternoon sun filters through the only window in the room, and I inch my desk closer so I can look outside while I work. Lorraine's voice rises peevishly and Gypsy starts to mumble, backing away, holding a hand to her cheek. Lorraine is a bitch and there's nothing to be done about it but retreat. It's impossible to calm Lorraine once you get her started.

I push my desk right up against the sill and lean over my typewriter. New Orleans and Jefferson Parish slide out before me, a steamy carpet of colors. The city shimmers and waves in the heat, the way a train looks as it goes off into the distance, blurred and unreal. The river seems only an arm's length away. Marshall told me if you fell in the Mississippi with your eyes opened, you'd go blind. I consider this sometimes, how danger waits in the most unsuspected places, how one topple into a river can make you lose sight of the world.

Today the levee is crowded. There's a Russian steamer and a Greek tugboat pulling through, their decks cluttered with uniformed men unable to form a familiar word on their lips, waving like crazy, like it meant something, like someone would remember their hopeful, foreign faces. The sidewalks are filling with people on their way home from work. The streetcar comes to a screeching halt before it nudges a car off the tracks.

I smell Lorraine's Juicy Fruit, her breath in my ear. She hovers over my shoulder, watching me type. I can't like Lorraine no matter how hard I try. I watch her sometimes, trying to find something to appreciate. She's got a cowlick and slightly bucked front teeth. She talks constantly in a big, spitty, gum-chewing voice.

"What is it?" I swivel on my chair to face her. It's Friday, she wants to go home though the office should stay open for another forty minutes. I'm not the boss, but Lorraine always appeals to me when she wants something. Then when I thwart her plans by dissenting, she punishes me for it, flicking her dry, bleached hair against my cheek, huffing away, mumbling about how uppity I am.

"Who died and made you queen for the day?" she says.

Gypsy rolls her eyes at me in sympathy. Gypsy is a poor typist and an even poorer speller. Last week she typed: FORTEEN BRAN NEW lo SPEED BISCICLES FOR SELL. Sometimes when I look up from my typewriter, I'm startled by her smooth, uncomplicated beauty. She's a mulatto with slim, leaf-colored eyes. She never looks at anything, she looks into things and past them, as though she were looking into another plane, the fifth dimension where her life is waiting for her, the real McCoy. Lorraine calls her a nigger behind her back.

Lorraine goes back to her typewriter and spells "gourmet" without the "u." She slams drawers shut, clomps around the office in her noisy clogs.

"It's Friday," she says again.

"Well, let's go home," I say, giving in. We pull plastic covers over our typewriters, lock desk drawers, pick up wads of paper on the floor. Lorraine watches from the door, chewing her gum, examining split ends. Her hair is too long, frazzled. One night I dreamed that I cut it off with fingernail scissors. It took a long time and I was in a sweat that she'd turn around suddenly and see me doing it.

"What you doin this weekend, Alice?" Lorraine says, chatty now that she's got her way and we're going home.

"Nothing much."

We walk down the hot sidewalk, threading our way through the crowds to the bus and steetcar stops. Lorraine chatters about her new boyfriend. Gypsy offers her cool profile to the winos lounging in front of an electronics store. They get on a bus together and disappear around the corner of Canal and Carondelet. I wait for my streetcar, watching shadows grow long on the sidewalk. I take my shoes off and feel the warm pavement humming beneath my feet.

The sun is a tangelo hanging just above the river, and the sky grows darker as the streetcar makes its way uptown. Along St. Charles Avenue the air is thick with the green smells of cut grass. I watch the grand houses along St. Charles Avenue blur past, Catholic schoolgirls in plaid uniforms loitering on the corners. By the time we reach my stop, night is hovering over the treetops, patient, waiting for its moment to fall. In this blue darkness, the air is heavy with ghosts. I can almost hear their voices, pirates mumbling curses, slaves gathering in the twilight to whisper mutinous secrets. The heat makes me slow and drunk with laziness. I look back over the housetops to where the sun is still hovering in the west, reluctant to give itself up to the night.

The city quivers with promise. Suddenly, I am lonely, alone, hangdog as I shuffle home. There is nothing so sad as leaving the night to others, as letting that promise pass you by. The humid air catches in my throat and I feel dizzy.

The neighborhood looks empty, abandoned. Everybody dressed for town, ready for dancing, dining, drinking by now. I push open the front door and walk through the shadows inside the house. I don't touch anything, don't make any noise. In the kitchen, I stop with my hand on the switch and sniff the air. Something strange has been here, I can smell it. A new scent, sharper in the darkness. Marshall. Maybe Marshall's come back, come back from the dead, waiting in the darkness at the kitchen table like he used to, smoking cigarettes, letting the night seep into him. I smell Spring, like a radish, peppery and red, pulled too early from the ground. My hand shakes as I reach for the switch.

Light, like a bright, yellow fan, breaks across the room and fills the corners. A wisp of smoke hovers over the kitchen table, a long cigarette ash dangling from its edge. But no one is here. The room is empty. The back door is slightly ajar, though I could have left it open.

I'm always forgetting to lock the doors. The door to the pantry is open, too. I peer into the dark stairs, call out Marshall's name, feeling foolish again, duped.

I walk to the back door and look at it as if it could tell me the truth of this: who has been in my house? Who is here? The curtains over the sink waffle with the breeze. I push the screen open and sit on the back steps and watch the yard grow dark. Dogs barking, faint music from a radio down the street. I smell bacon frying. Penny opens her screen and tosses grease from a pan into her yard.

"That'll kill your grass," I call to her.

"Oh, hi, Alice, what you doin, sittin in the dark all alone?"

"Just relaxing."

"Wanna beer or a soda pop?"

I walk down the steps and across the yellow grass to the short hedge between our houses.

"Betcha can't jump over them bushes," Penny says.

I back up a few paces and take a running start. The warm air is heavy and damp in my lungs. Just before I get to the hedge, I lose my rhythm and try to have myself by jumping higher, both feet in the air. I feel that flight for a moment and then my body gets heavy and I plunge, butt first, into the thick of the bushes. A branch skids along the skin of my back and pushes my shirt up to my neck. Penny laughs and calls for Boy to come and look.

Boy stays at the screen, cigarette smoke in a haze around his head. Languid and bored, he chews on a rasher of bacon.

"You can do that, cain't you, Boy," Penny calls. "Show Alice how you do it."

He studies the piece of bacon in his hand, then shoves

it into his mouth and wipes his hand on his shirt front, leaving shadows of grease. In a flash, he's out the door and down the steps. We look at each other for a long moment. Then he's moving, his body liquid with grace, his hair flopping in slow motion as he flies. He's over the hedge before I can take another breath. Penny claps and calls for him to do it again. And he does. I watch more carefully this time. How magic he is when he moves, his toes almost pointed, his face quiet with disregard.

"He can do it, all right," I say.

"Try it again, Alice," Penny coaxes.

"Nah. I thought you were gonna gimme a beer."

Boy sits on the step below me and Penny brings us beer. I stare at Boy when he's not looking, trying to make his face familiar. His hair is two-toned like a pecan, thick and wavy, cut short above the ears, but shaggy on top so it falls across one of his eyes like Veronica Lake's. His skin is soft and unlined, but there's something old about his eyes, tiny wrinkles and dark bruises beneath, a depth and craftiness in the pupils as though he's been looking at things for centuries, deciding upon their right to exist. The color of his eyes changes from brown to muddy green, like pebbles beneath murky water. He reaches down to pick up his can of beer and I notice his hands, the nails too long and yellow, the fingers quick and slim.

"I hope it rains," Penny gabs. "Maybe we'll get a breeze."

"I think somebody broke into my house." I watch Boy's face, listen to his shallow breathing. "When I came home tonight, there was a different smell in the kitchen. Cigarette smoke. And the door was open."

"Ooh," Penny squeals. "We was robbed once. They

took my radio and my TV, but they didn't take nothin of Boy's. Did they take anythin?"

"I don't think so. It was just a feeling I had. Maybe nobody was there, but the room felt different, you know what I mean?"

"Boy could go over and look around for you, just to make sure nobody's there," Penny offers.

Boy peers into the dark yard as if he's looking for something.

"That's okay."

"Gowan, Boy," Penny insists.

"Alice don't want me to."

"Gowan anyway."

Boy follows me around the hedge and up the back steps. I show him the open pantry door, the cigarette ash on the table. He moves through the house turning lights on, whipping open closed doors and yelling "Boo!"

"Nobody here," he says, holding empty hands up to show me. "But let's check upstairs."

"Oh, that's not necessary."

But he's already up the steps. I don't follow him; I don't want to look at my things through his eyes. I hear his footsteps above me making their way from room to room. Then he's standing at the top of the steps, looking up at the trapdoor to the attic.

"Lemme check up there," he says.

"Oh, don't," I say.

He gazes down at me, his eyes wet, unblinking. When I look into them, I think of quicksand. I think of what it's like to drown. He clomps down the stairs and follows me back to the kitchen.

"Yore granmaw give you this house, Alice? I remember yore granmaw. She used ta give me pralines at Christmas. Her darky made 'em."

His voice is low and lulling, but there's a bite to it, an edge of cruelty. He opens the refrigerator and takes out a can of beer for himself. His presence gives the room a hollow, quiet tension. Suddenly, I'm afraid. I feel as though we're waiting for something to happen, something dark and unexplained. The way a person waits in the night listening to someone weeping in another house. I want him to go but I don't want to be alone.

He hops onto the counter and sits, kicking his bare feet against the dishwasher.

"You like livin alone?" He strikes a match on the zipper of his jeans. "If I was Marshall I wouldn'ta run off like that. Where do ya spose he run to? Why would a guy like Marshall take off when he coulda had all this?"

I see the mocking curl of his lips; he cocks his head like a squirrel to gaze at me.

"I bin knowin Marshall a long time," Boy says. His lips are almost too red, a little obscene.

"Listen, Boy, thanks for your help, but I'm real tired . . ."

"Ahh," he sighs. He hops off the counter and comes toward me. He's looking into my eyes, moving closer, pulling me by an invisible thread into the dizzy, dark pit of his eyes.

"What are you doing?" I cry, turning from him, frightened by his closeness, his overripe smell. I remember something I'd forgotten, something buried deep inside my heart. Marshall, holding a fellow by his collar against a wall, talking low into his face, menacing a stranger who'd touched me. A stranger who'd placed his hand on my breast in a bar. The muscles in Marshall's arms, stringy and taut, as he held this fellow above the ground, his hands reddening as he clutched at the stranger's collar.

Boy puts his half-empty beer can in my hand, closing my fingers around it. I jerk away, but he touches my hand again with one long finger, tracing a vein.

"Alice," he whispers. He's smiling in the shadows near the door. Then I watch him trot across the lawn, his white T-shirt glowing in the dark. He picks up speed and vaults the hedge, his body as weightless as ash.

Three

*T*he azaleas hang fat and
heavy on the bush, shaking with dew. The sun is already
hot in the white sky. Somewhere above, an owl is hooting
slow, slow as a dream. The daylight is palpable and
comforting. After a night of unrest, listening to the house
settle, the sirens whining down Prytania Street, at times
convincing myself that Marshall was somewhere in the
house, eluding me.

When he lived here, he wouldn't answer when I
called. I'd walk through the house sometimes shouting his
name until I found him, in the gazebo, the garage, at the
kitchen table, in the guest bedroom lying on the taut
spread gazing at the ceiling. Marshall was not comfortable
with a home of his own. He didn't want possessions,
baggage to carry into the future. He wasn't attached to
anything, didn't own a thing he couldn't do without. He
was more at ease, more familiar with his surroundings, in
a motel than he was in our house.

Sitting on the back steps, I can hear Penny's new
Sears stereo. She's had it playing night and day, day and
night since she bought it last Thursday. I can hear the
faint wailing, the petulant whine of the country singers

she listens to, stories of desire, women gone awry, men gone away. Penny loves to sing. When she was a girl, she had ambitions. She used to sing "Love for Sale" when she auditioned at nightclubs in the French Quarter. Nobody appreciated her talent. The manager at the Blue Angel told her she had beautiful bosoms but didn't hire her.

Penny's voice rises above Elvis's as she sings along to "Kentucky Rain." There's a hollow, childish volume to her voice, something peevish about its pitch. She opens an upstairs window and shakes her bathroom rug, bits of lint and toilet paper floating to the ground.

"Hey, Alice, can you take me to the grocery? Boy took the car this mornin and I'm outa milk."

Penny's God-given, stick-straight hair flaps against her cheeks as she flails the rug against the side of the house. She has no makeup on, and she looks colorless, old. How did she get so fat?

"I'll be down in a minute," she calls. Her hair flops into her eyes, and suddenly I see Boy's face beneath the fleshy curves, the sublety of genes making a new design. Does Marshall look like his mother? I can't remember, can't bring his face to my mind's eye. Marshall, who's so large, so everpresent in my thoughts, has become faceless, disembodied in time.

I walk through the yard toward the garage. Inside, it's musty and dark. For a moment, as I'm trying to wrestle the garage door up, I'm afraid. I close my eyes and try to conjure Marshall's face. For a second, it rises, flashes across the stage of my mind, and hides in the wings again. I push hard on the door until it groans and slides up.

The car is parked amid a clutter of shovels, odd-sized pieces of lumber, old, broken appliances. I bought the car with Violette's money, the money she'd given me for college, before Marshall and I got married. The car belonged to somebody's grandmother, a friend of Marshall's, and I knew he wanted it. I bought it to please him. It reminds me of him. It's big and slim and you can't drive it fast. A white Bonneville. A harmless, blunt-nosed shark. I don't know why he didn't take it with him.

Before we were married, Marshall used to pick me up from work in the Bonneville when I was a waitress downtown. He'd park at the bottom of One Shell Square, the radio festive and lonely in the warm emptiness of those blue nights. I can see myself dressed in a brown pinafore too tight under the arms, my deep pockets heavy with coins, stepping from the hot, bright lobby of the restaurant into the cool, dank air, the smell of the river, clam sauce in my clothes and hair, my arms aching from the weight of so many trays of spaghetti.

We drive down St. Charles Avenue, go around Lee Circle, then down Carondelet past the all-night Walgreens on the corner of Canal. There are always sad, pinched-looking people there late at night, forged prescriptons for Dexedrine and Valium dampening in their hands. Marshall keeps his eyes on his reflection in the purple mirrors lining the Fanny Farmer candy store as we wait for the light to change. He sees himself better in the windows of cars and storefronts, he tells me.

From Canal, we tunnel into the French Quarter, past the Greeks selling disco records and digital watches and the Lucky Dog men wheeling big tin hot dogs filled with buns and weenies toward Bourbon Street.

On Iberville, we stare at the transvestites slinking along the edges of the bars. Then we drive along Decatur where women, and men who dress like women, come up to our windows, crooning, whispering, and Marshall knows them, their names, where they were born, where they sleep. Marshall knows everyone in this town: debutantes, Mardi Gras kings, winos, nuns, streetcar drivers.

We cut across the Quarter, buy a quart of beer at a carryout. Then we're deep in the Faubourg Marigny, the car bumping along the brick streets, the small houses looming, leaning off the curbs to follow us with their dark-paned eyes. The car sputters down Elysian Fields Avenue past the bakeries and TV repair shops, down toward the bottomland near the Mississippi where the avenue is ugly and bleak. It's so quiet here I can hear my heart beating, Marshall scratching a mosquito bite on his arm, the soft moans of a starlet from the X-rated movie theater across the street. The car gasps and rattles to a stop. We're out of gas. The bells in Jackson Square call the hour: two o'clock. The wind plays across the tops of the dying palms on the median. Marshall takes one last pull from his cigarette, flicks it, and watches sparks spit down to the gutter. He turns to look at me, his face strange in the shadows.

"What should we do?" I ask.

"Walk," he says and gets out of the car. I follow him down the wide sidewalk, stumbling on the uneven concrete.

"Where are we?"

He stops to light a cigarette, his hands cupped tenderly around the flame as though it were something to cherish. Ahead lies a small park, dense with trees, oaks and willows, a magnolia in the center, its blooms curled and brown. Marshall leans into a willow's trunk, rakes his hand across the bark.

"Elysian Fields," he breathes, his smile grave in the darkness.

I press my back against the tree, feel the scratchy bark through the thin cloth of my blouse.

"No snow, no cold, no rain. Where heroes go and live forever."

"Would you want to live forever?"

"Maybe." He drops the glowing butt at his feet. His face rises above mine, coming to meet me. I don't deserve this beauty, this bitter, scornful beauty.

"To never die . . . seeing everything again and again, the seasons changing endlessly, I couldn't stand it."

"And you don't got to," he says, his mouth against my temple. "You can live this minute like it's the first one or the last."

"The first one," I say. "I always want the first one so I can start fresh if I have to."

"I'll take the last," he says softly. He tugs the tail of my blouse, pulling me down beside him on the ground.

I feel my heart levitate, pressing against my skin, coursing electricity into my limbs. When I raise my hand to touch his shoulder, it seems to glow in the moon's light, shuddering with so much life. I see myself reflected in his pupils, miniature and whole, someone more real than me. A girl quiet and assured, suddenly beautiful and willing. I wonder how Marshall sees me. I run my hands along the grass. I smell the loamy earth, taste the tin of oysters on my tongue. His body dances inside mine until I'm moved, moved outside of myself and we are one and the same, Marshall, me, merged, melted down and shaped again into something new, just born, so rare and full of power we have no name.

I stumble through the blue night, past the squeezed-together houses painted sea foam, salmon, day lily. For a while, I've forgotten the facts that shape me, the color of my hair, my eyes, the sound of my voice. A stranger to myself, even my body has deserted me, each muscle singing, aching, my bones struggling to meld themselves together again. I try to keep up with Marshall who walks like a cat, his broad shoulders hunched, the muscles in his back sleek and fluid. I don't know where we are, where we're going, or where we've come from. I check to see if I'm wearing clothes, if shoes on my feet mean anything to me. See what Marshall does to me . . . see how easily he takes me, without a thought, without a struggle.

We reach Esplanade at dawn, the light rising pink and gold, the night trailing behind us like an old tin can. At a service station, we gather money to buy gas. Marshall offers our beer to the attendant.

"What's that?" he says, looking over into an open space in the parking lot, where two trucks with Tennessee license plates and a couple of lumpish, bearded men are lounging on their bumpers, drinking out of mason jars and watching a skinny woman throw batons of fire into the pale sky. My head is muddled with smoke. I watch the fire spin as if I had just discovered it and could never tire of its newness, its power and insolence.

The attendant takes the change Marshall pours into his hands and gazes across the parking lot.

"Doan know," he mutters and walks away.

Marshall lopes across the lot, his arms flung in welcome, his hair copper in the early morning light.

"Whatcha'll doin?"

"We all got a show over at the Five Hundred Club tomorra night," the woman calls, her voice high and piping like a child's. She snatches a rod of fire out of the air just above her head and twirls it like a smalltown majorette, around her back, through her legs, then in front of her chest. She walks toward us, her kid with crossed eyes and matted hair following behind her so close he bumps his nose against her bottom when she stops. He rests his head against her hip and peers at me crookedly. His mother drops the batons, still lit, and rolls her naked foot over them until the fire dies.

"I swalla swords, too."

"How?" Marshall asks.

"You kin learn, you kin learn," she assures him. "I started when I was fourteen, unravelin wire coat hangers and dippin em in whiskey. The whiskey's fer sanitation. Then I jist keep stickin it down my throat till it gits to my gullet. It ain't hard. Just takes practice."

Her skin is so pale, her skull seems to show through, a gray shadow beneath. She tugs at the tangled hair of her little boy, gently pulling her sooty fingers through the rats in his mop. Behind her, a man burps and throws a mason jar into the tall weeds behind the truck.

"Hey, kids, ain't you never heard of the Flamin Bunny Galore?"

Marshall laughs. I search my mind, feel like somewhere in my life I lived in Tennessee, drove a truck on all the roads that lead to Rock City.

"It's me!" she screams with delight. "It's me!"

*   *   *

Standing just inside the garage door, my hand cool on the hood of the car, I've forgotten where I am. I'm surprised it's midday and not dawn, not two years back when life was something different. Regret waters in my mouth as bitter as an unripe lime. I watch a black man walk through the backyard and stand at the screen waiting for someone to answer.

"Hey!"

He turns sharply, squints through the sun to see me coming across the dead grass.

"You live here?" he says. His voice is deep, rich, thick as pudding. He has skin like soft dirt packed hard and smooth. Beads of perspiration line his forehead and upper lip, and he dabs at his mouth self-consciously.

"Who are you?"

"Percy Diamond. My granmaw worked in this house." He gestures at the house, his eyebrows arched over his dark, perfectly round eyes. His lips are full, boyish, almost smiling.

"Cleva Pear?"

"Yeah, Cleva Pear."

Violette had a picture of Cleva in one of her diaries. A photograph like a school picture, black and white, a young Cleva in her high school graduation dress. She had a wide mouth glossy with lipstick, black hair like cotton candy, round eyes, like her grandson's, large and moist, too wise in a young girl's face.

"She's dead," Percy Diamond says. He wipes his sleeve across his brow, hiding his face for a moment in his armpit. I see his pink palm. I've never spoken to a black man before who wasn't a streetcar driver, a waiter in a restaurant, or just somebody brushing past me on the street.

"I'm sorry."

He gazes at me for a moment, his lips moving slightly as though he's whispering a secret to himself.

"I live in the boardin house behind you." He points with a long finger. "Is you related to Miz Violette?"

"Yes."

"Maybe you got some work for me. Lawn mowin. Handyman stuff."

He waits, fingering change in his pocket. I can't tell how old he is, maybe thirty, maybe still in his twenties. He begins talking again, nervously, embarrassed to have asked for work.

"I work at the Acme Oyster House. In the French Quarter. Do you know it?"

Out of the corner of my eye I see Penny storming down her back steps.

"I don't have any money. I can't pay you to do any work. I wish I could . . ."

"No, no," he says quickly. "I got to go now. I'm late for work."

He reaches forward, takes my hand in his long fingers and presses something into my palm. The movement is so graceful, I don't take offense at his strange touch.

"Cleva took this from Miss Violette. She wuz feelin bad bout it fore she died. I tole her I'd bring it back, but I ain't got round to it till now."

I open my hand and look at the brooch he's pressed into my palm. A pale pink cameo with a cheek chipped off, lint from Percy's pocket caught in the bent, brass clasp.

"Wait." I'm embarrassed for him. I want to give it back, but he's already through the bushes and climbing the outside stairs to the third floor of the boarding house.

Who's that nigger?" Penny says crossly, tweaking a curl of her wig into place. Today she's a brunette with a mini-beehive.

"He's not a nigger."

"Looked like a nigger to me," she says. "Now, Alice, I hope you won't git mad at me, but Mama wants to go to the grocery with us. She has to buy hairpins at the supermarket."

I can hear her pantyhose whispering between her thighs when she walks around the side of the car. She slams the door and waits for me to get in. When we get out on St. Charles Avenue she dumps a Band-Aid tin full of newspaper coupons into her lap and riffles through them.

"Just honk the horn a coupla times," she says when I pull up in front of her mother's little crackerbox house. "She ain't deaf, yet."

I honk the horn, thinking of Violette and how she would have insisted that everybody get out of the car to escort her down the stairs. After a few moments, an old lady in a faded purple wool coat creeps out of the house and down the front path. She has greasy, marcelled hair.

"Why's she wearing that heavy coat? She's gonna die in the heat." It makes me hot just to look at her. Penny glances up but goes back to her coupons. Mama Lapere makes her slow shuffle to the car.

Mama Lapere works the door handle. She can't seem to press hard enough to release the latch.

"Get in, Mama," Penny sighs impatiently. "You remember Alice, my next-door neighbor."

Mama Lapere waves a weary hand at me. She pulls shredded Kleenex from the sleeve of her coat and blows noisily. She has left the car door open and I have to get out and go around and close it before we can leave.

"I'm gonna buy me a big ol barrel of Strawberry Swirl ice cream. Remind me, Alice," Penny says.

We march single file into the supermarket, first walking idly up and down the aisles until Mama Lapere stops in front of a display of children's school supplies. She reaches out a prehistoric hand and drops a package of 100 Crayola Crayons into the large pocket of her coat.

"Penny," I whisper, "what's she doing?" Penny isn't paying attention. She's fingering packets of chocolate cherries. Mama Lapere shuffles up to the counter with her hairpins. The clerk is a high school girl, her face freckled with pimples.

"How we doin today?" she says brightly. Mama Lapere digs a small leatherette coin purse out of her pocket and counts the pennies one by one.

"My, won't yore hair look pretty in these pins," the clerk exclaims, examining the package of ordinary brown metal pins. Mama Lapere looks up at her and smiles. She's nearly toothless, her gums gray and rubbery.

Penny and I walk Mama Lapere back to the car with her hairpins, the stolen Crayolas, and a two-pound sack of chocolate cherries which Penny has already opened and is eating hurriedly as though we're going to take them away from her. Mama Lapere gets into the back seat with all the windows rolled up to wait for us.

"Your mother stole some crayons in the supermarket," I tattle.

My mother used to pin a homemade tail on me when I tattled. Penny glances at me as if I'm somebody else's kid hanging on the wrong mother. She picks up a jug of milk and checks the date.

"Alice, you forgot to remind me about that ice cream," she scolds, a much greater transgression than stealing a pack of crayons.

Once we get the groceries packed in the trunk of the car, we drive down St. Charles Avenue toward Mama Lapere's house. Mama Lapere allows us to open one window. The car is rancid with heat and the moldy smell of Mama Lapere's old coat. I press down on the accelerator, but the car doesn't want to move very fast. I put my foot all the way to the floor and the car roars back at me and limps a few feet forward. Penny's eyes grow big.

"Mama, what did you do to this car while we was in the supermarket?"

Mama Lapere looks up and frowns.

"Sounds like we got a hive of bees under the hood," Penny says. She turns in her seat to glare at her mother. I can see Mama Lapere in the rearview mirror, defiantly scratching her nose.

"Penelope," she says in a voice so much like Penny's cartoon voice that it's eerie, "I bin sittin here like I always do and if this automobile ain't doin like it's sposed to, it ain't no fault of mine."

"There *is* something wrong with the car," I say. Smoke filters in thin blue streams from under the hood.

"We better get to a gas station," Penny advises.

I inch the car along, a line of fidgety traffic building up behind us, honking. Finally, we spot a Tenneco station on the corner of Carrollton Avenue. A black man sits on the curb by the office door. He's wearing a pink shower cap and there's a yellow bird perched on his shoulder, pecking birdseed from his narrow palm.

An attendant rushes out of the garage and gapes at us. He's wearing blue overalls with pants too short at the ankle.

"Hey, girls, better get outta that car fore it blows up!" he hollers in a squeaky, elated voice. I scramble out and rush to the other side to help Mama Lapere. I scuttle her over to the office and sit her down on the curb next to the man with the bird.

"Lady, you goan suff-cate in that getup," he tells her, plucking the sleeve of her wool coat with his skinny fingers.

"Do somethin!" Penny screams at the attendant. "I got milk in them bags in the trunk. I'll give you a dollar if you git them groceries outa the trunk."

The attendant rushes into the garage and comes back with a long, green garden hose. He sprays a great gush of rusty water at the hood of the car until the smoke drowns.

"It's the transmission," the black man shouts. "You ladies need a new transmission." The bird hops up on his shower cap and back to his shoulder again. I open the trunk and start taking out grocery bags.

"Give her a hand," Penny orders the attendant. He waddles over and peers into a bag.

"This car gotta have a new transmission right away, miss," the attendant tells me.

"How much?"

"Bout six hundred dollars, miss."

"Alice!" Penny screams in horror. "How you gonna pay for that?"

The black man shakes his head and makes a clucking noise in his throat. Penny disappears into the office to call a cab.

"You wanna take this cab home with us, Alice?"

"You got to leave this car here, miss," the attendant says.

"Stop calling me 'miss'!"

I follow him into the office and sit on a cardboard box filled with motor oil, listening to Penny and her mother quarrel about the cost of the cab. Penny wants Mama Lapere to take the streetcar home so the fare will be cheaper. "You don't got no groceries," she reasons in a shrill, petulant voice.

A Checker cab drives up to the pumps and honks impatiently. I help Penny put the groceries in the back seat. Penny and her mother get in the front seat beside the cab driver, who looks sweaty and irritable and disgusted with this turn of events.

"Come on, I got yore groceries!" Penny hollers. But the cab driver doesn't wait. He pulls out of the station, squealing tires, bounding down the street as though he's about to give chase. I can see Penny and her mother arguing, the backs of their heads bobbing in disagreement.

The black man gets up from the curb and comes to stand beside me. He seems to have a hunchback under his shiny black suit jacket. I close my eyes a moment, shutting out the bright sun glinting off the chrome of the broken-down cars in the station parking lot. When I open them, the bird is perched on the shower cap again, pecking at nothing.

"How come you're wearing that shower cap? I've seen lots of black men wearing shower caps."

"I'm givin myself a treatment." He laughs. "My rug is goan feel like silk, ya know." He pulls up an edge of the cap to show me his glistening, nappy hair.

Four

$\mathcal{M}$r. Whistle, the mailman, is standing on the front porch digging into his mailbag when I get home from the gas station. Mr. Whistle is from Martins Ferry, Ohio; he recognized my accent the first time we met, and it pleased him to think he could still identify an Ohioan after thirty years of living in New Orleans.

"Hi, Mr. Whistle." I'm carrying a grocery bag Penny forgot, and butter is melting through the bottom making my hands greasy. I put the bag on the step to look for the house key.

"Hello, Missus . . . Bettonville," he says, curiously sullen. His pumpkin face is sunburned and peeling. He gazes at me as if he's never seen me before and hands me my mail: a flier from a pizza parlor.

"I never get any mail. I haven't even gotten a bill in more than a month."

He stares at me, his eyes fixed blankly on my face. This stare alarms me. He looks dazed and confused as though he might faint.

"Is anything wrong?"

"This ain't a communist country," he says smartly,

brushing past me down the steps. He points at the sticker on his leather mailbag, the eagle, the postal service emblem. "This is the United States of America."

I unlock the door and step inside. I can smell the egg I fried this morning, the cigarette I smoked, the warm, dusty air filtering sun through the hallway. I wander into the kitchen and put the groceries away.

Out the open kitchen window into the backyard, I see two fellows standing over a brick barbecue pit behind the boarding house. One is Percy Diamond. I watch him make his way across the grass and into my yard, stumbling over a rusted rake on the platform of Marshall's unfinished gazebo. He catches himself before he falls and looks around sheepishly to see me watching him. I unlatch the door and let him inside.

"I never bin in this house," he says. "Cleva said I'd break sumthin. You got any charcoal? We're tryin to start the barbecue."

He looks about him, places a long palm on the kitchen table like he's trying to read its vibrations. He's wearing Army fatigues, camouflage clothes to hide himself from the enemy.

"Sorry, no charcoal."

He walks through the kitchen and into the foyer. Sunlight, checkered from the panes in the front door, falls at his feet, illuminating dust motes in a chaotic swirl.

"Cleva wuz always talkin bout Miz Violette's room," he says, gazing toward the staircase. "She said Miz Violette had a bed like a queen. And these little bottles a colored water in the windas. Miz Violette tole her these bottles brought magic light in the room."

"The bottles are still in the window. Violette's room

probably still looks the same as when Cleva worked here. You want to see it?"

We walk up to the second floor. Percy stands, hesitant, in the doorway of Violette's room, my room. I try to remember what I thought when I first saw this room, when I realized I would sleep and dream here. For a second, I remember Marshall's face the first time he came here, his eyebrows raised, a hint of fear in his eyes. Violette lingers in this room like a troubled ghost, keeping vigil over her belongings. Marshall was never comfortable here under Violette's watchful eye. Perhaps I should have moved the furniture, masked its feminine scent, bullied the room into our own likenesses. I still move gingerly here. Each night I fold the old lace spread down gently as though it might fall apart in my hands. I avoid touching the silver brushes on the mahogany dresser, dust around them so as not to disturb them. The double bed is fitted with bright cotton sheets that I wash and line-dry every Sunday. There's a lace canopy draped over the carved posters of the bed, and a white satin dust ruffle. The bottles of colored water are faded, but still cast purple, green, yellow, and red shadows on the shiny wood floor.

"Jest like a queen." Percy smiles.

When we move back into the hallway, Percy notices the trapdoor to the attic at the top of the stairs. A frayed foot of rope with a looped handle hangs from the ceiling.

"I've never been up there," I tell him. "Can you reach the rope?"

His arms are long, and when he stands on his tiptoes he can just catch the bottom of the loop. He pulls hard and the stairs unfold. I rise behind Percy into the dark, musty room. We have to stoop until we get into the middle of the attic because of the sloping eaves. Dim light sifts through small windows along the front of the house. The room is empty except for an old leather trunk, a battered yellow armchair, and a refrigerator box. I push back a veil of cobwebs, squat before the leather trunk, and tip back its creaky lid. The trunk is papered inside with pink flowers and smells of mothballs and dying roses. It's empty, but there's a false bottom. I tug at the rusted clasp until it pops open. Dozens of scarves, filled with the roses' unendurable breath, seem to rise in the air like flimsy phantoms, specters of iris and narcissus, tulips in colors running with water.

I glance back at Percy to see if he's noticed Violette's memories crowding the room, but he's hunched in front of one of the little windows, watching a pigeon strut on the ledge outside. Cobwebs are draped over the eaves above his head like Spanish moss. I take a scarf from the trunk, a long, canary yellow silk with bright tulip heads scattered about the edges, and wrap it around my neck. Violette's perfume settles upon me as soft as snow.

"Lookat this," Percy says. He's beside the yellow chair now, staring at a footprint in the dust on the floor, the size of Marshall's foot, with the tapered toe of a cowboy boot. We lean over and study it like it was a dinosaur print sunk in bedrock. I remember when Marshall and I went to buy those boots in a dark and gloomy secondhand shop near Rampart Street stuffed to the gills with moth-eaten feather boas and fur coats, faded ball gowns, yellowed negligees and bed jackets, old Mardi Gras costumes, crumpled high heels, and hats swinging from the ceiling—pillboxes, Italian felt bowlers, derbys, and stovepipes like trapped birds fluttering against their chains.

No aisles: you had to squeeze through choked racks of shirts and pants and suit coats stained with perspiration, smelling of sweat and stale cologne and cigarette smoke.

Marshall found the boots in a box near the door. They were soft with age, a deep caramel color, tiny eagles stitched into the sides with gold thread. A perfect fit, they belonged to him, had been made for him, had been waiting all their life for only him. The man at the desk, sunk in a rubble of crumpled paper, paste jewelry, and faded soda pop cans, watched us, his eyes as small and perfectly round as pennies. Strange eyes, lashless, pupil-less, a dirty yellow hue.

"Yes, yes," he said when Marshall brought the boots to him. "These are yours. I knew it right away." He stroked them, fit the heels into his palms and held them aloft. His skin was the gold of olive oil and as smooth and wrinkle-free as a baby's or a dead man's. His hands trembled as he put the boots in a grocery bag.

"I saw heaven today," he said, his smile beatific, his teeth perfect and white and too small in his wide mouth.

"Is it nice like they say?" Marshall asked.

"Oh, yes," the man said, peering through Marshall, a film masking his eyes.

"What do you want for the boots?"

"Nothing, nothing. I saw heaven today."

Marshall placed ten dollars on the counter and we went outside.

"What's wrong with him?" I asked.

"Junkie," Marshall said. He sat down on the corner to slip on his new boots.

"He gave me the creeps." I shivered in my thin jacket. It was January, rainy and gray, the cold knife-sharp

49

and damp. Marshall squinted up at me, sighed, and shoved a hank of hair out of his eyes.

"Don't make judgments, Alice. You're always lookin at the wrong things bout people. Everybody can't be what you want. You got to be kind."

Wind whistled around the corner of the building, scattering dead leaves and trash through the cobbled street. Marshall stood slowly, stamping his boots.

"Right now, you look this small to me." He held up two fingers, an inch of air between, that was me.

"My husband's."

"You got a husband?" Percy says. I kneel on the dirty floor and look closer. For a moment, I forget Marshall's not downstairs, that he's not coming home, that he's not just around the corner making footprints everywhere.

Percy reaches inside the refrigerator box and brings out a jar. He holds it out to me. It's pickled okra, homemade, with a small, hand-drawn label picturing a black woman in a red dress holding a basket of tiny green okras. Cleva Pear has signed her name, a chicken-scratch scrawl, to the bottom of each label.

"Pickled okra." Percy sighs.

We take a couple of jars downstairs and stand at the picture window in the living room, chewing okra and looking out on the street. Mr. Whistle rustles through the Hooters' mailbox. He looks behind him and snaps the lid shut. Percy holds a jar up to the light and watches peppercorns swirl to the bottom.

"Here come that woman," he says.

"That's Penny. She lives next door."

"I seen her," he says. "I got to be goin."

I hold an unopened jar of okra out to him as he turns to go.

"Why're you going?"

"Doan do no good to be hangin round white people like that. I had to tell you sumthin else—there was these two guys at yore back door this mornin. I seen em from my winda on the third floor. I doan know if they come inside cause I got called away to the phone."

"What time?" I follow Percy's hurried retreat through the kitchen.

"Bout eleven. I got to git charcoal. I got to go now."

"'Yoohoo, Alice!" We hear Penny letting herself in the front door. Percy's already outside and halfway across the yard.

"What did they look like?"

"I'll tell you later," he calls.

I hear Penny clomping through the hallway into the dining room.

"Here's yore groceries," she says, huffing and puffing as though she's toted them across mountains to get them here. She dumps the bag on the kitchen table and turns to leave.

"Where are you going?"

"I gotta git ready for my date. I told you, I'm goin with Mayo to the Pontchartrain Amusement Park."

"Oh, yeah. But it's only three o'clock."

"I gotta do my nails, don't I?" she squeals. "What you doin tonight, Alice?"

"Nothin."

"Boy's sposed to be home." She actually winks at me. "Ya'll could pop some corn, watch TV together."

She slams the front door behind her, and I go back and sit down in the empty kitchen, wondering how I'm going to pay for that car. How am I going to get Marshall's car back?

The dark comes late. I walk back through the easement into Penny's yard. Her backyard is a mess. She pays a boy to mow the front, but she's too cheap to let him do the back. There are probably weeds ten years old back here. I get scratches and chigger bites every time I walk through it. As I near the house I can see Penny's head in the kitchen window. She's wearing an enormous strawberry blonde wig like a golden tower on top of her head.

"You should change your name to Cassandra," I say, peering at her through the screen. She leans over with a grunt to wipe grape jam off the toe of her shoe.

"How come?"

"You look like somebody named Cassandra. I think Cassandra was a goddess. She could tell the future."

"I don't like to know the future."

False eyelashes encircle her shiny brown eyes like a wreath of stars. She's wearing a purple chiffon dress, belted at the waist with a gold tasseled rope that looks like something you'd use to tie back velvet curtains in a castle. On her feet are tiny, gold mules.

"When's Mayo coming?"

"Any minute, honey," she says absently, gazing at her reflection in the kitchen window.

"You look beautiful."

I follow her into the living room and we sit on the couch to wait for Mayo.

"Boy ain't here," she says. "He went out tonight. I tole him you might stop by, but he has sumthin to do . . ."

"I didn't come by to see Boy. I came to see you all dressed up. Where did you ever find a couch like this?" The couch is made of a velvety material, red and black checked like the tile floor of a bathroom. There are cigarette burns on the arms.

A car grumbles down the street and Penny busies herself over her accessories. She checks her earrings, straightens her hose, rustles through her purse counting lipsticks. Mayo is fifteen minutes late.

"It's a sofa bed," Penny mumbles, patting the couch. "What are you gonna do bout that car, Alice?" She pushes her tilted wig in place.

"I don't know."

"Well, I cain't worry bout it now," she says grumpily, checking her wristwatch again.

"Is he ever late?"

"I don't remember." She plays with the plastic raspberries on her earrings, holding herself apart from me. I must appear shabby in my shorts and T-shirt.

"What's wrong?"

"Nothin, honey." She's so absentminded it's making me irritated.

"Why don't we have a drink while you're waiting?"

Penny has a rolling bar. I get up and wheel it out into the middle of the living room, feeling like the hired bartender at a flopped party. I like this bar. It's a marvel of modern convenience. The sides are covered with indoor-outdoor carpeting so you can leave it out in the rain. I make Penny's version of a martini with a cherry instead of an olive.

"Boy's daddy was a car salesman," Penny says gloomily, looking out the darkened window. I stop shaking the martinis and stare at her. She's never told me anything about her husband before.

"He sold three Buicks in a day once. He run off when Boy was five, and I sold my diamond ring for twenty-five dollars just to pay the rent. I hope I ain't never that poor agin."

"Why don't you call Mayo?"

She looks at me from beneath her penciled brows like a dog that knows he's done something bad but doesn't want to be punished for it.

"So, you see, Alice," she continues soberly, "I know what it's like to have a man run out on me."

She's trying to make me feel bad because she's feeling bad. Mayo is now forty minutes late, and she wants me to feel the rejection of that, too. She's always ignored Marshall's disappearance. She ignored Marshall for the most part when he was around, although once she told me she thought he was cute. Of course, Penny uses the word "cute" to describe just about anything she doesn't have much use for. Two days after Marshall left, she gave me a big lecture about other fish in the sea. We were drunk at Gino's Lounge and I tried to imagine just who those other fish might be. But I couldn't imagine being with anybody but Marshall. And I still can't, though sometimes I try to pretend there's another face beside me in the dark, another hand on my leg, another body breathing slow and easy at my side.

"Better off without him," is what she said to me that night. But am I? I don't know that yet. I don't know what that means. Would I be a better person without Marshall?

Smarter, prettier, happier? I don't know. It hasn't come true yet, if it's supposed to.

"You can call, Alice," Penny whispers feverishly. She takes the martini from my hand and gulps it like she's dying of thirst. "You can call!"

"You mean Mayo? Call Mayo? Aw, Penny, I don't know . . ."

"Please, Alice. I got to know. I cain't just sit here waitin all night."

"Aw, Penny, what would I say? What if his wife answers?"

"Please, please, Alice. I'll dial the number. I won't make a peep. You could say, 'Let me speak to the man of the house,' like you were takin a survey or sumthin. Then we'd know if he's home."

She picks up the phone in the living room and dials Mayo's number before I can protest again. Then she hurries into the kitchen to listen on the extension. I hold the phone to my ear, listening to the sharp ring. A kid answers.

"Can I speak to the man of the house . . ."

I hear Penny pick up, her light breathing in the receiver.

"You mean my dad?" the kid says.

"Yes," I say, feeling cruel and little. The kid drops the phone with a clatter.

"Don't hang up," Penny whispers.

"Daddy!" the kid screams.

Then we hear Mayo's voice. "What?" he hollers impatiently. Heavy footsteps, and a noise like someone ripping up a newspaper. He picks up the receiver and shouts, "Hello, who is it?" I can't speak, his voice is too loud in my ear, making me forget what I meant to say. I put the phone back on the hook.

When I go into the kitchen, Penny's bent over the sink, sobbing into a dish towel. Thick berry paste is crusted on the towel and she scratches idly at it as she cries.

"Don't cry," I say. Penny and I have never hugged. My hand rises instinctively to pat her on the back.

"Oh, Alice," she wails, "let's go out and have us a good time. Let's buy some drinks . . . have us a good time." She hiccups violently, a hand covering her mouth, a hand at her breast. I give her a spoon of sugar and the hiccups stop.

"You better fix your face."

One of her eyelashes has come unglued and dangles along the side of her nose. I sit on one of the flamingo chairs around her kitchen table and wait for her to come back from the bathroom.

Her eyelashes intact, her pantyhose straightened, she emerges from the bathroom and swipes a fat tear from the corner of her mouth. I wait for her to lock the door behind us and we walk into the hot night to the streetcar stop.

Penny turns heads on Bourbon Street. She cuts a bold figure in purple chiffon, her false blonde hair coiled and glistening, dangling to her shoulders like links of pale, fat sausages. She walks like she's modeling in a fashion show, posing on street corners. When she pauses to do this, I don't know what to do with myself. I seem to be in her way, blocking the view.

"Let's go to Saint Peter's and get our cards read," she

says. We stand on the corner of Bourbon Street watching two Negro boys tap dance. Brothers, scruffy and tattered, little slugs or washers glued to the bottoms of their shoes. The smaller is doing the dancing, tapping his heart out in the middle of the street, his bottom lip folded over in concentration. He's not as good as he is determined. Penny watches the boys and eats her third eggroll from the Takee Outee Chinese fast-food shop.

"Not Saint Peter's, Penny. It's so sleazy in there."

"It ain't sleazy, Alice. We kin git our fortunes told."

Saint Peter's is a nightclub in a talcum pink building on a quiet block of Bourbon Street away from the tourist bars. Inside, ladies of the evening loiter around the bars while freshly shaven men from Tupelo and Dallas stand in the doorways, stunned by the garish glory of it all—the velveteen wallpaper, the delicate antique carvings on the staircase—the clinking of glasses and silver bracelets ringing in their ears.

Penny has a hard time deciding whether we should sit inside the piano bar or outside in the courtyard. At the piano bar, a couple of Navy pilots are slumped over the piano, singing in loud, horrible voices. Penny grabs my hand and pulls me into the ladies room. Two beautiful whores lean against the sinks talking about aspirin. I turn away from them and pretend to be interested in the hand dryer machines while Penny uses the toilet.

"I take me bout eight to ten aspirins a day," one of them says, lifting her perfectly coiffed head to study her slim neck in the mirror. Her face is gaunt, her cheekbones jut beneath the purple haze around her eyes. "I get the cramps bad."

"Don't never take none when yore drinkin schnapps,"

the other advises. She's small and plump and blonde and looks like she's been fed on fried pork and potatoes all her life. She's tried to hide large freckles under a smooth slather of makeup. "You won't remember a goddamn thing bout where you bin." Her laughter careens around the tile walls. She leans down in front of a perfume machine and drops a quarter in the slot. Her freckled breasts pout from the confines of their Quiana bodice and make me think of Corinthia. Bedraggled but feminine in her tight gypsy dresses. Sexy. Corinthia's behind twitches like a metronome when she walks. Tick-tock, tick-tock. Who taught her that walk? Was it something she was born with or something she had to learn? Like these whores who've taught themselves to move like hula dancers, to smell like the night and flowers, to play pretend at passion and desire. I catch sight of myself in the mirror. Always a surprise. I look as though I've combed my hair with an eggbeater. I come closer, inspect my face in the dusky glass. Not so bad. I have high cheekbones, a noble nose. But the lips are too thin, the eyes too narrow. What would it be like to be beautiful? A woman who stops traffic? What would it be like to wake each day knowing that whatever you put on would only gild the lily?

But Corinthia's not what you'd call beautiful. She's downright homely, if you ask me. Though she's got *something*—that walk, those soulful, slightly myopic eyes, a way of pushing her tangled hair from her face that says a thousand things: come here . . . go away . . . I want . . .

Penny comes out of her stall and watches a spray of imitation Shalimar shoot into the crevice of the woman's breasts. When the women turn to leave, she examines the machine with real interest.

"Did you ever see anythin so handy!" she exclaims. She drops a quarter in. "I'd like to have me one a these at home." She tries to get down to the spray of Tabu, but she's not quick enough, and it squirts all over the shoulder of her dress, leaving a heavy, musky wet spot. From out of nowhere, she begins to wail like an animal left to sleep in the garage.

"C'mon, don't do that. I thought you wanted to get your fortune told. That spot will dry and you'll be sweet-smelling in no time." I yank toilet paper off a spool and help her wipe mascara from her cheeks.

The courtyard bar is crowded. Penny wiggles through a herd of college boys to the last two stools at the bar.

"How come you ain't goin to college no more, Alice?" She settles her big haunches on the tiny stool and raps her long fingernails on the bar to get the bartender's attention.

"I didn't like it." This isn't true exactly. I liked the smell of new books, the way you could befriend a stranger in a minute, the flurry of bodies in the cafeteria, the noise of the bells when classes ended, the sense of collusion. Marshall drove me to college one day during the first month of school. He looked older, remarkable; no one would mistake him for a student. For a moment, I felt sorry for him, so out of place. He stopped the car in front of the student union and smiled at me. But I knew I would betray him there. I knew I would grow comfortable in a world where he would never belong. And I didn't want to belong to it either. I wanted to live where Marshall lived, inside the night, roaming the back streets like a gypsy, friendly with the club barkers, a pal to all the waiters and waitresses drinking in the Absinthe Bar in the wee hours after work, the Latin women who read your palm and handed you towels in the restaurant bathrooms, the fat twin brothers behind the counter of the po-boy shop down the street from our house. There was a world beyond my own that I wanted to know, and if I didn't live in it with Marshall, didn't take that chance, I felt I'd never know anything.

I got back into the car and looked at Marshall's profile chiseled against the gray sky. I felt brave for the first time, as though I'd saved someone—myself, Marshall, it didn't matter—but someone who's lost now, misplaced, maybe never to be found.

The man on the stool next to me turns to look at us. He's about fifty with a mass of healthy white hair and a dark beauty mark on his cheek.

"One time me and Harry Glasscock was in a night-club in Vegas and we jest missed seein Wayne Newton around the corner at the roulette tables," Penny chatters. She exchanges winks with the man beside me.

"I didn't know you'd been to Las Vegas."

"Oh, honey," Penny giggles, a real veteran of the hot spots in the world. The man gets up and wriggles between us. He has wide, womanish hips.

"I bin to Vegas lots of times," he tells Penny.

I look around the courtyard. Above us on the second floor are bedrooms and offices. Three whores make an entrance down the spiral staircase. Above them, the sky is black and filled with stars. Through the crowd, I can see the top of the card reader's turban bobbing among a sea of heads.

"There's Albert!" Penny cries, leaning across the man, her breasts pushed up against his hands. "Hey!"

Albert sees her and nods politely. My gaze drifts around the bar again. Behind the dance floor is another bar. Men sit on stools staring at the couples dancing. They're all wearing hats, except one. I stare at the hatless one. He looks familiar. He puts a cigarette between his lips and holds it there, the smoke drifting into his narrowed eyes. Boy? It's Boy. In black jeans and a black T-shirt.

"Madam, to what do I owe the pleasure . . ." Albert is saying behind me. He's wearing a polyester gypsy blouse with billowing sleeves and some sort of scent too flowery to be men's cologne. The skin on his face is dry and thin like the skin on a clove of garlic.

Penny makes introductions. She doesn't know her new boyfriend's name, so he makes a big show of handing out his business card. Rodney Buckles, Attorney at Law, Birmingham, Alabama. Penny introduces Albert as Swami Albert. I look back beyond the dance floor for Boy. A woman leans on his arm, her hand on his neck, one leg flung over his thigh.

I offer Albert my stool so he can lay the tarot cards on the bar. He shuffles expertly and turns each card over carefully, murmuring impressions. I slip through the crowd and get on the other side of the dancers till I'm standing close enough to Boy to hear what he's saying, to smell the woman's perfume.

"What you doin here?" He pinches my arm too hard. I look at the welt and try to rub it away.

"I'm with your mama."

He's very drunk, his lids heavy, his mouth wet and

sloppy. He slouches against the bar, trying to keep his balance. The woman stares me down for a few moments and finally turns away to lean against the man on the other side of her.

"Lemme buy you drink, Alice," he slurs, slapping the bar with his palm to get the bartender's attention. "Hey, hey . . ." He catches a guy by the sleeve. "Meet Lumey."

Lumey is Boy's pal with the Dixie horn. He's at least six feet tall with wide, fleshy arms like radial tires. His head is shaped like a pear, but flat on top, his pale hair short and bristly. Little pig eyes in a fat, stupid face.

"Get Alice a drink," Boy commands.

"Whut's she drink?"

"I dunno, jes git her sumthin."

Lumey shuffles off, and Boy looks back at me, musing upon a private joke.

"I'm celebratin."

"What? Did you get a job?"

"Oh, I got lots of jobs." He laughs, throwing his head back. His teeth look long and dangerous, the canines slippery. "Lookat this ring I got." He flashes his hand in front of my face. A square band of gold with a big blue stone. It's too big for his slim finger, and he slips it off so I can get a better look.

"Who's M. J.?" The inscription inside the band says, "M. J. to B. J. Semper Fi, 1966."

"Gimme that." He snatches it back and drops it into the pocket of his jeans.

"I'm goan git me a woman," he whispers, leaning toward me. "Doan tell Mama I'm here. Doan tell Mama you seen me, okay?"

His breath smells of rum and oranges. He burps noisily and scrubs his face with his hands. When he looks up at me, his eyes are watery, weak. His skin is drained of color, but his lips are ruddy, almost indecent against his pale face. Fumbling for another cigarette, he slips off the stool and wanders drunkenly onto the dance floor. I follow because I've got no place to go.

"You tailin me, Alice?"

He stumbles through the dancers, bumping hips and shoulders, and into the foyer where we can hear the piano, the Navy pilots still singing.

"She always comes here when Mayo stands her up," Boy mutters. His eyes are shiny, too bright, glinting like chrome. "You doan have to wait on her. She likes to find her own way home."

He opens the door and stops, running his hand along the fuzzy fleur-de-lis wallpaper. His lips curl into a bitter smile.

"Ain't you afraid a me, Alice?"

"You want me to be?"

"Oh yeah," he says, "that would be good." And then he goes, the door standing open without him, the night closing around him. I can hear music in the street, a saxophone whining a sad song to the fat air.

Penny, Albert, and Rodney Buckles are looking serious over the cards when I get back to the bar. Rodney's hand rests on Penny's shoulder.

"Penny, I wanna go home."

"Yeah, honey," she says, and waves me away.

Albert looks up from the cards. He's so short, I could

rest my chin on top of his turban. His eyeliner is smudged in a crude circle around his lashless eyes. His smile startles me; the anger and impotence lurking behind it are a surprise.

"Call me in the mornin," Penny says.

"I seen a thunderin herd of horses when I looked at you," Albert is saying, peering into my face. He stands too close, the turban pressing against my cheek. "Things is gonna change for you, big changes."

Suddenly, I can barely breathe, and I'm jittery to be released from this place. But I don't know what to say, what gesture to make that will grant me escape.

"Thank you, Swami Albert." I reach out to shake his small hand as I back away.

Swami Albert smiles again, like he's just saved my life.

Bourbon Street is deserted. Half-eaten corndogs, plastic cups, and a pair of broken chopsticks float along a viscous green stream of disinfectant in the gutter. I step off the sidewalk and walk down the middle of the street. A barker stumbles off the curb to lure me into his club. I'm alone in the street. The barker is just a boy; he has dark, sleepy eyes, a baby's face, tattoos along his arms like blue sleeves.

"Come ere," he whines, and puts out his hand as if to lead me onto a dance floor. "Where you goin, little miss, come in here where it's cool. See the show, have a drink. We got S and M here, Sneakers and Makeup!" He laughs, hoarse from cigarettes, sniffling as though he's got a cold. I walk around him.

"Stupid bitch," he mutters.

I stop at a pay phone and look through the yellow pages for the address of the Acme Oyster House. It's only two blocks away on a little street off Bourbon. I take a stool at the bar and look for Percy Diamond. The shucker tells me he's gone on break and won't be back for ten minutes.

Oysters jiggle in a bed of rock salt on the bar in front of me. They're cool and slippery in my mouth. Penny told me that Mayo once ate 167 oysters to win a contest at a bar in the Irish Channel. He got a hundred dollars and bought her a certificate for a "Day of Beauty" at the Cosmetology School. The "Day of Beauty" included a manicure, pedicure, hair consultation, and eyebrow waxing. The student beauty operator got overzealous with the wax and Penny came home eyebrowless.

Percy bangs the saloon doors of the Oyster House open and gets his rubber apron on before he notices me at the bar. His body is awkward behind the narrow lane. He knocks liquor bottles with his bony elbows, catches a little bowl of lemons with his hip, and it spills to the floor.

"What about those two guys at my door this morning?"

"Jest two guys." He pulls rubber gloves up to his wrists and takes up his oyster knife, opening the shell on the first try. "White boys. One had wild brown hair—I think I seen him someplace before—the other was sorta fat."

"What were they wearing?"

"Dark stuff. Black. I doan remember. They was at the back door and then they was over to the kitchen winda fiddlin round. I din't have no binoculars."

Wild brown hair. Black clothes. Sounds like Boy. But what's he doing? Why would he try to break in? He can't get rich robbing me.

"Hey, what's yore name?" Percy says. He scratches his nose and leaves a stripe of oyster grit along his cheek.

"Alice."

"Alice in Wonderland. I seen it on TV. You got some trouble, Alice?"

"I don't know. Sounds like it."

"White people always got troubles jest like on TV."

Five

The streetcar is almost empty. I sit up front watching the two other passengers in the driver's long, rearview mirror. One is a young black girl in a cheerleading outfit. Her hair is standing on end like she's seen something scary, and she's bleached a blonde skunk stripe down the middle. The other is a white guy, about forty, wearing a faded aqua cowboy shirt with gold oil derricks embroidered on the breast pockets. He's talking to himself. The girl takes out a cigarette and leaves it unlit between her sullen lips. The streetcar is lit like a little glass box moving through the dark of the city. The driver seems reckless, careening around the corners, braking too abruptly when he thinks someone is waiting at the stop ahead.

Two stops before mine, a man gets on and sits down across from me. He's wearing cowboy boots covered with silt. When he looks up, I see it's Whitey, a friend of Marshall's. His white hair is tucked beneath a dirty fishing cap, his eyes hidden by the brim.

"I know you," he says, studying me.

"I'm Alice."

"Oh, yeah," he says, but I can see he doesn't yet know who I am.

"Marshall's wife."

He takes the cap from his head, his long hair falling to his shoulders, and gazes at me, his eyes knowing, remembering.

Whitey took us to the courthouse the day Marshall and I were married. He complained the whole way downtown. His truck needed new tires; he was afraid he was going to get a flat. There weren't any parking spaces around the courthouse; someone would tow his truck away. Why did we have to get married, anyway? he wanted to know. Couldn't we just live together?

Marshall stared out the window. I could smell the sweet, candyish odor of his hair, the whiskey on his breath. I was afraid to touch him, he seemed so alone. *Here,* he said finally, and took my hand, placing it over his heart so I could feel its slow, insistent beat, the promise there.

"Well, Alice," Whitey says, "how you been?" He looks around the car because he doesn't want to look at me. He's trapped.

"Fine. You still working for that construction company?"

"Sure," Whitey says, suddenly captivated by a plastic wrapper stuck to the bottom of one of his boots. The car seems terribly quiet. The guy in the cowboy shirt continues to talk to himself: "Why didn't you let me be?" he says.

"I spose Marshall's bin makin sum kinda money on them rigs," Whitey says. He chances a look at me.

"What?"

"I heard bout him workin outa Morgan City, but I ain't seen him in a long while."

"Marshall?" I say, as though learning his name.

"If I din't hate the water so much, I'd be workin there, too."

I watch the driver fly past my stop. Maybe Whitey and I will be stuck here all night, riding round and round until I get some answers. I reach up and pull the rope for the next stop, but the driver keeps going, hell-bent into the dark night. What is Whitey saying? I hear rushing in my ears like the sound in a conch shell. Marshall on the rigs . . . well, of course he is. Why wouldn't he be? Where else would he be? What did I think? Did I think he was pining away for me someplace? Mexico, Australia? He's on the rigs. It's so easy, so logical. The car jolts to a stop and Whitey stands up. I think I'm going to cry, but I can't let Whitey see me. I have to wait, one more minute, one small minute, until he's gone.

"Tell Marshall to gimme a call when he gits in town." He picks a pimple on his chin before he goes down the steps and disappears around the corner on Carrollton Avenue.

We're two miles away from my stop now and I don't even have thirty cents so I can get off and catch another car going back downtown. I dread sitting here for another hour going around the city, sunk in this horrible quiet. Crying. I can see myself in the windows wherever I turn, another character lost on the streetcar, another stranger to avoid.

Marshall, you shit. How many people know about you being on the rigs? Could you have told me you were going and I didn't hear you, or did I forget? Was I sleeping when you gave the news? That's when you often told me things, when you thought I was sleeping. Your body clammy against the sheets, your tongue restless with scotch or beer or both, so you could let your heart open and speak, hesitant, vaguely disgusted with yourself, but certain I was three sheets to the wind and none the wiser. But I was listening. My body plump and ruffled for sleep, my breathing timed to a dream's rhythms, my eyes shut gently, fluttering slightly, believable as a dog twitching on the carpet. Remember, you told me about your father, how he made you dig that grave in the backyard between the lime trees so he could bury himself with a case of Dixie beer and the Mason's handbook? Remember telling me about the first girl you made love to, a sorry thing, a mission of mercy for a tattered little belle who'd been beaten silly by her older brother for wearing a miniskirt to church? Remember confessing to me about despising your mother, shuddering at her touch, the sound of her voice, suspecting that you'd always hated her, repelled by her scent and her cloying love? No. I didn't forget or sleep through the news of your leaving. Every word that's escaped from your mouth has been engraved on my heart, fondled, pored over, learned like a hymn. And still, I'm always the last to know. You deny me simple facts, little truths, the comfort of knowledge. From the beginning, I've had to pry you open like a stubborn shell to get to the gist. Maybe you do it to spite me, to deprive me of the solace knowledge brings. But how can I fault you when you've never had need for solace, never lived through the grim months of learning to go it alone? Because you've always been alone.

Six

On the rigs. A fellow can make some money on the rigs. I wonder what Marshall's been doing the weeks he's not working. Does he come into town? Most of them do, living hard and fast for a week or two, deprived as spinsters but wild as bobcats. I take the streetcar downtown and get off at Lee Circle on a hot, August Monday. The pavement is white and seems to shimmy beneath my feet as I walk the five blocks to the Magruder Oil Company. There are other oil companies, but Magruder's is the one I've heard of, the one some of Marshall's buddies have worked for. The receptionist eyes me suspiciously. She pretends not to see me and busies herself looking through the top drawer of her desk.

"Could I speak to Mr. Magruder, please?"

She almost laughs.

"Mr. Magruder ain't here. He ain't never bin here."

"Who's in charge?"

"Mr. Lasko. You gotta make an appointment."

"Couldn't I speak to him now? It's really important."

"Sorry. He ain't here either. You got to make an appointment." She switches her electric typewriter on and fiddles with the space bar.

"Isn't there somebody I could see?"

"Nope."

A man in a black suit and dark sunglasses comes out into the anteroom from the back of the office. He seems to be on his way to an early lunch. He leans over the receptionist's desk to look at her calendar, poking his long nose down the front of her blouse to look at her breasts.

"What can I do for you?" he says absently, flipping through a pile of mail. He's bald and his head looks like he's just oiled it.

"I'm looking for somebody."

"How can we help you?" He puts a hand on my back and guides me into his office, closing the door behind us. On the desk is a gold-plated name card: Bernard Lasko. His walls are covered with pictures of rusty derricks in the sea and maps of the gulf floor. He looks at me expectantly, blinking round, wet, gray eyes.

"My husband," I say. "I think he's working on one of your rigs."

Mr. Lasko doesn't seem to think this is an unusual situation. He takes a large black book out of the top drawer of his desk.

"Name please."

"Marshall Bettonville."

"Marshall," he says without inflection. "Bettonville. B's."

Marshall's got to be in that book. I can't be wrong this time. It makes too much sense.

"I've got a Marsh Bettonville here," Mr. Lasko says finally. "We sent him down to Morgan City over five months ago. He's been working for us five months . . . and twenty-two days."

So, here you are, Marsh. A person bearing half a name, the rest lopped off.

"Morgan City," I say.

"Anything else?" Mr. Lasko says, clapping his hands together without making a sound.

Morgan City. A continent away.

On Friday, after work, I get off the streetcar in front of the Tenneco station.

"Your car's done, miss," the attendant says. He's eating potato chips, and there are crumbs in the corners of his mouth.

"How much?" Somebody starts banging on a tail pipe in the garage, drowning out his answer. "What?"

"Six hundred thirty-nine dollars and forty-two cents, miss."

"Can I pay half of it now and take the car home?"

"Gary," he hollers, tipping his chair on its hind legs so he can see into the garage. "Can she pay for half the car and take it home?"

"You knucklehead!" Gary hoots. "She cain't drive home in half a car!"

The attendant laughs, spewing bits of potato chips on the desk.

"You cain't drive home in half a car . . ."

"Okay, I'll come back."

"We got a five-dollar-a-day parking charge, miss."

"Stop calling me 'miss.'"

He adds five dollars to the bottom of my bill and smiles.

* * *

At twilight Violette's house is hushed and solemn. I try to imagine her walking through these rooms, running a finger along the mahogany dining table testing for dust, or sitting in her chair in the living room watching the traffic go by.

I go into the kitchen and fry myself an egg. I consider doing laundry, watching television, but I'm too bored and restless. Standing over the sink, I pour a full can of beer into a tall glass. I tip my head back and pour it down my throat to see if I can drain it all in one gulp. I get three-fourths of it down without choking, swallow, and finish the rest. After a big burp, I feel a little better. I wash the dishes and hear noises in the backyard. Boy's standing on the platform, kicking a two-by-four onto the grass. He tests the timbers that hold up half the gazebo roof, leaning against them to see if they'll give.

"Alice, yore goan be a happy girl," he says when he sees me coming toward him across the lawn. As I get closer, I notice he's wearing a suit and a pressed pink shirt. He's even got loafers on.

"How come you're dressed like that?"

"Had a business meeting," he explains, raking the hair from his brow. He looks older in these clothes, less threatening somehow.

"What are you doing here?" I sit down on the platform and look up at him.

"I hear you got car trouble." He hikes his pants up and squats beside me. His face is close to mine; I can see his pores, stubble on his chin. He smells of cologne. He takes a cigarette out of a pack inside his shirt pocket, offers me one, and lights them both—from his mouth to mine, the butt a little damp. This intimacy is troubling, and I

74

turn away so he won't see me when I wipe my lips with
the back of my hand.

"Mama says yore car broke down."

"They fixed it, but it's gonna cost over six hundred
dollars."

"Look," he says. He pulls his pantleg up and a gray
sock down and shows me a thick sheaf of money taped
around his ankle. He picks at the tape with his long
fingernails and shoves the money toward me. I touch it,
but I don't pick it up. Twenty-dollar bills, crisp and
green, fluttering with a small breeze.

"I'll loan it to you," he says, picking a mosquito off
his face. When he takes his hand away, there's a red streak
of blood on his cheek.

"For nothing?" I say.

"For nothing. Pay it back when you can."

"I don't get it."

"I'm loanin you money." Irritation tightens his voice.

"Why?"

"Maybe you'll do me a favor sometime."

I look at the money again. I pick it up, count it. One
thousand dollars. I can pay for the car tomorrow. I can go
to Morgan City.

"I can't take it." I push it away.

"Yes you can, Alice." He sighs. He takes my hand
and folds it over the bills.

"Could I pay it back in installments? I'll only borrow
six hundred."

"Pay me back any way you want. Jest don't tell
Mama I give it to you."

"Why?"

"Jest don't."

The darkness is coming, our shadows loom long before us. I look across the dead grass at Boy's dark image, the silhouette of his arm as he flips his cigarette into the bushes. The money is warm and dry in my hand. I look back at Boy. The expression on his face is almost sweet, a hint of satisfaction on his barely smiling lips.

"Thank you."

"For nothin," he mutters. He puts a hand on my leg and pushes himself up. Then he goes back through the bushes and into his house, turning off the kitchen light behind him. I sit for a while in the quiet holding the money in my hand.

"Mr. Rubio ain't gonna like you takin half a day off, Alice," Lorraine whines. She pulls a hank of hair in front of her face and inspects it, cross-eyed, for split ends.

"Yore gonna tell on her, ain't you, Lori?" Gypsy laughs.

"No, I ain't gonna tell on her, but I don't think she should be surprised if she gits fired."

"Well, it's Friday," I say. "There's not much to do."

Lorraine's still pouting when I walk out the door.

There's a forty-dollar parking charge on the car bill. I pay it off with the twenties Boy gave me.

I get in the car and gun it; the black man in his shower cap watches from the door of the garage. The engine roars, and the car bounces over the curb into the street. Morgan City is an hour and a half southwest of New Orleans, but I drive slowly through the city, past Jim's Fish Store, an art deco bowling alley, across the Mississippi River Bridge and down into the dangers of Algiers, a forgotten, violent neighborhood along the river.

Before I know it, I'm through Marrero, Westwego, Raceland, and finally Houma. Houma is close. I'm going forty-five, reluctant to get where I'm bound.

What was I thinking? Why did I imagine I could just drive into Morgan City and find Marshall waiting for me on the street corner? Morgan City is bigger than I expected, more real, more peopled. Perhaps I thought no one in the world would be in Morgan City today except Marshall and me. Once past the city limits sign, I drive badly, racing up to stop signs, pouncing on the brakes. I pull into a gas station and look through the phone book for the address of the oil company. The gas station attendant can't tell me how to get there. He's from over in Raceland, he tells me, and there weren't any jobs in Raceland so he took this job in Morgan City because he's real good with his hands, everybody said so in his high school shop class . . .

I get back in the car and the attendant follows me, still talking about why he doesn't know his way around Morgan City. He pats the side of the car as though it were the flank of a horse. That's when I decide to find Magruder's office on my own. I can't bear to ask anybody else.

For two hours I drive aimlessly, frightened by each approaching street sign. At four o'clock, I finally blunder across the street the company is supposed to be on and it's only two blocks from the gas station where I began. I park in front and look at the building for a while. Maybe

Marshall will be inside by some enormous coincidence. I have no speeches ready.

The receptionist looks so much like the receptionist in New Orleans, they could be sisters. She says the same things, fiddles with the space bar on her typewriter, thwarts me in the same ways.

"You've got to help me," I plead.

She shakes her head sadly.

"I got some things to finish up here, then I'll see."

She sits straighter at her desk and rearranges a bunch of peonies in a little glass jar. Then she takes the coffee pot down the hall to the ladies room to rinse it out. She comes back and sharpens six pencils. It's five minutes till five now. Finally she disappears into the back office. She's gone for more than ten minutes. I'm certain she's going to close the office without telling me where Marshall is, and I start to cry, quietly, angrily.

When she comes back, she's carrying a big black book just like Mr. Lasko's. She looks at me with disgust, and untouched by my tears, takes her time looking through the book. She doesn't ask for his name.

"His name is Marshall . . . no, Marsh Bettonville."

"Ah. He just got off the rig yesterday." She slaps the book shut and locks it in one of her desk drawers.

What does this mean? She stares at me and I stare back; if only I could ask her what to do. I imagine confiding in her. Telling her about Marshall, appealing to her sense of romance. She flicks an ant off the petal of a peony. If only somebody would tell me what to do!

"Is there someplace he's likely to go?"

"Lots a them stay at the International Motel when they only got a day or two between assignments."

"Where's that?"

"Oh, down the street there." She becomes vague again. "Anybody could tell you."

I go back to the car and rummage through the glove compartment looking for a piece of paper to write a note on. I've had enough for one day, I'm thinking. I'll just write Marshall a note and be done with it. This is cowardly, but I can't help myself; it will give me time to think, or rather, not to think about what I should do. I find a blank restaurant check under the front seat with a faded map of Dogpatch, Tennessee, on the back. I'll just write this note;

"Dear Marshall."

Now what?

"Dear Marshall,

Please call me. How are you? I'm okay. Please write or call."

I almost write down the phone number and address and that makes me sad enough to cry again. But what's the worst that could happen? Marshall would leave me. But Marshall's already left me. What could he possibly do to hurt me that he hasn't already made a stab at? It feels good to cry, and I haven't had a good cry for what seems like a long time.

The International Motel is a long, low-slung building, dingy and lonely, sitting on the edge of a deserted old highway just outside Morgan City. It looks abandoned in the heat of the day. There are a couple of junky cars in the parking lot, a dented Airstream trailer decorated for newlyweds—shaving cream dried on the windshield, old tin cans tied to the bumper. The office is painted hospital green, faded magazines strewn across the top of the rickety coffee table, a straw mat, gritty with sand, covering the linoleum floor. Behind the desk, a woman in a black CPO jacket drinks something pink from a plastic mouthwash bottle.

"I'm looking for my husband," I say. "The people at the oil company said he might be staying here."

Her eyes are clouded by cataracts, blue and milky as opals. A small fan behind her on the windowsill blows hot air at the back of her head, making her white hair stand up on end. She blinks, and for a moment I suspect she might be blind.

"His name is Marshall Bettonville. Is he registered?"

"Oh," she mutters and peers absently at the registration book on the desk in front of her. "I think he's here, sweetie." Her voice is a whisper, kindly and muddy with age.

"Could I see him?"

"He might be in Egypt." She coughs for a few moments until she can get another gulp of the stuff in the mouthwash bottle. I wait, sweating in the tiny office. The last sun of the day is too much in this room, filling the corners, splaying across the counter and floor with a cruel brilliance.

"Egypt?"

"Thas the economy room," she explains. "Down in the basement." She mumbles directions, points a crooked finger down a dark hallway. I start down the corridor, but stop in a bathroom to splash water on my face. There's a machine that sells condoms—french ticklers, and something special called a black zombie that promises to make your partner a prisoner of your will. I dig a quarter from my purse and buy one of these, hoping to amuse Marshall, thinking it will be something to talk about if all else fails.

Out in the hall again, I find a door that leads down some metal steps. I come into a dim, long room with pipes exposed along the ceiling. The walls emit cool, gassy fumes. I run my hand along the damp wall until I get to a door with a pyramid painted on its cracked surface.

"Marshall?" I push the door open with my toe.

It's a dark room, windowless. A TV sits on a chest of drawers, its picture tumbling back inside itself and filled with static. The bureau is the color of sand with tiny, painted asps slithering out of the drawers. The bed is shoved up against a damp, dark wall, a waterbed. I stare at it for a moment, wondering, because I've never seen a waterbed in a motel room. There aren't any suitcases in the room, no clothing draped about, no signs of life except some spotted plastic cups, and the purple crushed velvet spread bunched up at the bottom of the bed.

The bathroom door is angled out into the room like the side of a pyramid. The toilet's gently overflowing, and the floor is wet. I jiggle the handle and it stops. With a loud slam, the door shuts behind me. I stand next to the toilet, listening. Someone has come into the room. I hear another door shut, the swish of water. Someone sitting on the waterbed. Dead still, my hand clutching a cheap purple hand towel on the side of the sink, I wait, afraid to move. A few strands of Marshall's red hair ring the basin.

A cheap eyeshadow compact lies open on the counter. The waterbed gulps and swallows.

I tip the door open and peek out. A girl is sitting on the bed with her back to me, humming to herself. She's got long yellow hair, as dry as toast, a frail back like a child's. She rolls a can of Coca-Cola across her brow.

"Is this Marshall's room?"

"What you doin here?" Her voice pierces the air, makes the lamp by the bed shudder. She whips around to face me, the cola can cradled against her face.

"Where's Marshall? Is this his room?"

Her eyes are big and lopsided with lashes that blink and swish like false ones. A scar separating her cheek from her mouth turns pink as she glares at me. Her fear makes me angry. I feel the blood come back into my limbs.

"Marsh," she says. "He ain't here."

It's terrible, but I want to slap her. I can even imagine myself reaching out to do it, my palm tingling against her cheek.

"When's he coming back?" I'm still standing halfway in the bathroom. I can see myself in the mirror over the bureau across the room. It's like seeing myself in a movie.

"Who wants to know?" Only the bed is between us. She places her hands on the flat bones where her hips should be.

"I'm his wife," I say, hoping this will have some impact, feeling sort of gleeful in the telling. But why I should want to lord anything over this dirty, sluttish little girl is anybody's guess, and it doesn't give me too much pleasure.

"Oh," she says. When she pops open the can of soda, a sticky spray hits her face but she doesn't wipe it off. "I didn't know he got a wife." She gazes steadily at me with her big, over-lashed cow eyes.

"This TV is broke," she tells me, watching the picture flip. She goes over and twists the knob on the set until it comes off in her hand. "There," she grins, "I broke it good."

"Who are you?"

"Ettie."

"How do you know Marshall?"

"We worked on the rigs together, but I got kicked off. Marsh got hisself in a fight over me," she says, proudly.

I don't think I want to hear about this. I feel very tired all of a sudden. If the sheets looked clean, I'd lie down on the bed.

"They goan let him back, but he's got to pay a penalty fee. They ain't goan let me back. How you like this room? We coulda stayed in Norway where they got these cute little fireplaces, but Marsh wanted to sleep on the Nile." She nods toward the bed where she and "Marsh" have lain together. I have to sit down in one of the throne chairs for a moment when I imagine this.

"You wanna see the swimmin pool they got here?"

"No." I think of Marshall and Ettie in the bed together.

"You really his wife?"

What a pathetic creature she is! I almost feel pity for her scrawny little legs, her flat wrists, her sweet, dopey eyes. But I have little pity to spare right now. I'm keeping it all for myself.

"He told me he was goan take me to Las Vegas," she says sadly. "You spect he will now?"

"It's anybody's guess." I try to picture Marshall and this girl in Las Vegas, sticking quarters into slot machines, standing in the bald sun beneath dying palms and neon signs. I had daydreamed about the time I would see Marshall again, the things we would say to each other, the acceptable excuses he would give me, the resurrection of my pride. But this is not what I expected. I feel confused for a moment. Time seems strange. How long have I been here? What time could it be? How long have I been looking for Marshall? A few hours? A couple of days? Months? I don't know where I am. My skin is hot and tight as though it's the wrong size, like when you get somebody else's coat from the coat-check girl at a restaurant and realize it's not your own.

"He didn't say when he was coming back, did he?"

"You never know bout Marsh." She nods sagely.

I sigh and wonder what to do. I can't wait here forever. But what else have I got to do? Marshall will come home in his own good time, when he wants me for something; there's no need for me to search him down like a bounty hunter. He'll resent it, be angry at me, and I'll go away with nothing, no answers, no apologies, no clue how to continue, how to live my life without him. And every time I've tried to second-guess Marshall, I've been confounded.

"You want a rum and Coke?" Ettie asks. "I got me a little bottle in the bathroom." She goes into the bathroom and comes back with two dirty glasses and a cheap bottle of rum. She pours a little Coke in the bottom of the glasses for color and three fingers of rum on top.

"What you lookin for Marsh for anyway?" she says, handing me my drink. The rum is harsh. I shudder and take another big gulp. If I get drunk, this will seem easier.

"Just to see him."

"How long you bin married?" she persists.

"About a year and a half."

"That's a long time . . ."

I can't be in this room any longer. It's dark and hot, and I feel cranky. I drain my glass and set it down on the wooden arm of the chair.

"I've got to be going now. Thanks for the drink."

"You want me to tell Marsh sumthin for you?"

"You can tell him I stopped by." I'm hurrying to the door, banging my knees against odd pieces of furniture. Ettie slithers off the bed to follow me.

"Hey, what's yore name?"

"He knows my name."

It's dark outside. The stars are hiding in a thicket of murky sky. Junebugs scratch in the dusty bushes around the pool. The water looks black and secretive, oily and deep as a bottomless pit. There's a man sitting down by the diving board, smoking a cigar. The burning tip glows on and off like a beacon. He doesn't look up when I pass. I climb over a cement wall between the pool and the parking lot and make my way toward the car. Moths fly circles around the pink neon sign, diving desperately between the glowing letters. There are two or three more cars in the lot now, but the motel still looks empty and closed and far away from the rest of the world.

I lean against the car door and scrape gravel from the bottom of my shoes. I can hear a light breathing sound, even and full, and I imagine it to be the night, sighing rhythmically. I open the car door and almost sit down on his head before I notice him.

Whiskey, wild chives, dark, damp, dirt. Marshall. I can smell rain, then, coming, sweeping north from the gulf. My head is spinning with the smell of him and the rain, as clean and sweet as a lime, threatening to wash that memory away. There's a half-eaten hamburger on the dashboard, and without thinking, I reach for it and put the soft bun between my lips.

He sits up slowly, bones cracking, his spine complaining. The red shock of hair that drops over his forehead is pushed up stiff like a little soldier from the way he's been sleeping. His cheek is imprinted with the vinyl pattern on the car seat. All of these things I notice before it dawns on me that Marshall is here. Yes. Here is Marshall. Long-lost Marshall. Everything moves in slow motion, our eyes opening wider to take each other in. The slow climb of his arms as he reaches for the ceiling to stretch. My jaw works over the hamburger.

"Ha!" he says, his voice taking its time to reach me over months and months of absence. He watches me chew. "You hungry?"

Yawning, he presses his palms against the ceiling, making the stringy muscles in his arms pulse. His T-shirt is damp under the arms with sweat.

"What you doin here?" He looks like Howdy-Doody with his hair all pushed up like that.

"Nothing much," I say, chewing calmly. The hamburger is still warm. I wipe my mouth with the back of my hand. "I met your girl."

"Oh, Ettie." He grins. "She's a chippie, wouldn't ya say? Ain't that the right word? Chippie?"

Chippie. Jailbait. Forlorn. Pathetic. All words that could describe her. He leans in close to me and sniffs.

"You've bin drinkin rum. I can tell from ten paces what somebody's bin drinkin."

"It's a talent," I say. "Too bad you can't find a market for it."

"That's right," he says, scrubbing the sleep from his face with his hands. "I got all kinds a talents nobody has a use for."

Marshall yawns again, showing me his handsome teeth. I always liked those teeth, liked to watch him bite down on a piece of bread or meat. I remember my Aunt Mamie advising me once, "Look at their teeth. If they have good teeth, you can be sure somebody paid some dentist bills and they haven't been eating candy for breakfast."

Well, he looks the same. The same teeth, the same haircut, probably the same dirt beneath his fingernails. I look him over as though I'm identifying his body in a morgue. There's the scar over his left eye from diving into an empty swimming pool. A small almost imperceptible blue X on the inside of his wrist from the initiation into a gang he decided not to join. His eyes are slim and tapered like pumpkin seeds, the pupils dark, almost blue-black like cobalt. They never change color or lighten in the sun. They never widen with surprise or narrow in contempt. Expression in Marshall's face comes from someplace hidden, someplace intangible and solely animal. But he's a handsome animal, a big cat of some kind.

"Can't you give me something . . . an explanation, an excuse?"

A small bird lands on the hood of the car and is more surprised than me to find itself there. It seems to have tumbled off the roof of the motel. It is the smallest of dull, brown birds. I watch it wobble down the slope of the hood and tip lightly over the fender.

"'Ask me anything," he says generously.

"Why don't you call Lucy Nell? She thinks you're dead. She thinks I murdered you, chopped you in little pieces, and threw you in the Mississippi."

"I'll call her." Marshall groans.

"I want proof. I got change here. Let's find a pay phone."

"Not now. I cain't do it now. I got to be ready for that."

"You'll never be ready," I say, and suddenly feel like I'm going to cry. I'm so tired. My eyes are heavy and puffy with tears. The last bite of the hamburger is stuck, thick and damp in my craw. "She hounds me," I squeak, my voice betraying me. I feel so sorry for myself, and a moment ago, I was doing so well, so calm, so flip. "She comes over every day and takes things back: her washing machine, that cross she nailed to the front door . . ."

Marshall puts his hand on my knee and I swat it away. I don't want him to touch me. No telling what will happen.

"She still does your laundry, you know. She took all your clothes one day. She folds and irons everything, even the underwear. Thinking you're going to walk in one day. God! It makes me crazy!" I cough and turn my face to the window so he can't see me.

"You make me feel mean," he says, his mouth a stiff, white line. "That's what you do real good."

"Oh, that's fair," I blubber. My nose is growing bigger, redder, taking over my face; I can barely breathe. Marshall fishes a flask from his back pocket and hands it to me.

"This'll make you feel better."

I take a big drink and feel the whiskey make its way down, hot and acidic. My crotch dampens with relief, my arms and legs go limp as water.

"I'm gonna throw up," I manage to gasp as I wrestle with the door handle. My stomach leaps into my throat and I lose the hamburger and everything else to the gravel at my feet. I'm too weak to close the door, and I lean my head back against the seat, my face smeary with tears.

"You're making me too sad." Marshall sighs. "And I was feelin good. I was feelin good when I saw my car. I knew I didn't have to go down into that little motel room cause this was a better place to be."

"This is my car now." I watch him from the corner of my eye. He takes a drink from the flask and breathes deeply.

"You shoulda been smarter, Alice. You shoulda never let us get married. It was a mistake and you hate mistakes. You shoulda been smarter."

"I didn't force you to do anything. Maybe you shoulda been smarter."

"I don't mind makin mistakes so much, not like you. That's why *you* shoulda known better."

"That's too easy," I cry. "You always make things sound so stupid and easy."

"It's true, though. You're always tryin to make sure

you get everythin right the first time." Marshall drinks
from his flask, looking off into the night as though he's
talking to himself. "But you weren't takin me into account, how I got to make BIG, grand mistakes with all
the glory of a parade, flambeaux carriers and a marching
band. I got to have everybody pointin their fingers at me
and holdin me up for example. But that's not you, Alice.
No. You hate a mistake like you hate not knowin the
truth. I spose that's what you're doin here now. You want
to know the truth of it. But I can't give it to you. I don't
know what the truth is. I don't even care. You're a hard
girl to make happy. I always hadda be on my toes."

"I'm not so hard to make happy. I don't want so
much. I don't know what you're saying," I whisper, my
throat raw and closed. I reach for the whiskey, thinking it
will calm the scratch in my throat. "I don't understand
what you mean about the truth. You know why you left.
You could tell me if you wanted to. I'm not so hard to
make happy."

"You're always tryin to plan everythin out, Alice, so
it'll go smooth. And you don't care to wait and let things
be, to let them happen naturally. You want to know the
true meanin of things before they come to their finish. But
life ain't like that. You got to wait for things to finish
before you can know what they mean. You can't always do
things right the first time, no matter how much studyin
you do. The problem with you is you can't stand to fail, to
fuck up . . ."

"But who likes to fuck up?" I wail.

"I do!" Marshall hollers. "I like to fuck up better'n I
like to do good. It makes me feel more at home with
myself. It confirms the nature of things for me. And doin

good don't last long enough. Once you do somethin good, people expect you to do it again, or keep it up. But once you do somethin bad, it lasts a long time. People remember. It's got more stayin power."

"You're full of shit!"

We'll wake the whole motel. We'll bring this brawl into the middle of the street where everybody can see. I want to hurt him, to punch or slap him, to scratch and see blood. I've never before wanted to twist an arm, to feel a bone snap.

"You don't love anybody or anything!" I scream because in my mind this is the greatest sin of all, to have nothing to love, no one to sit witness for. But then, in the still that sits vigil outside my words, I hear the word "love" ringing like a sassy bell, tinny and mocking. It's the wrong word in this place. The wrongest of words. It doesn't belong here and has been abused by the conjuring of its presence.

"Oh, love," Marshall sputters impatiently. "We're not talkin bout love. We're talkin bout the truth. Maybe I never did love you. Maybe I don't love nothin at all. But you didn't really love me either. You were lookin at somebody else, dreamin bout somebody else in your stupid girl dreams. You did me a wrong, Alice, tryin to make me into somebody else. Don't you see that this is an old story? We aren't rare. This happens every day. We aren't anybody special. People have been doin this to each other forever. It's so old, it stinks."

Rain falls on the windshield, big fat drops making clean holes in the yellow dust. I listen to the slow sound of it hitting the roof of the car.

"What are we gonna do?"

He looks surprised. He turns to face me and places a hand on my forehead like a father feeling for fever. You *did* love me Marshall. I know you did. But you're right, we aren't special or rare. This *is* an old story, and I deluded myself into thinking we invented something new.

"It's all right, Alice," he whispers. "You'll learn to live with it. For now . . . you just keep tryin to find out the truth of things and I'll just keep fuckin up big. If you need someone to blame, you can count on me. That's what I can give you now, Alice. Blame me."

I can feel his breath on my face, his warm mouth, a hand circling my neck. The rain patters on the roof. The moon's face is swallowed by gray clouds racing across the sky. It's so dark in the car, I don't have to close my eyes not to see. Yearning grows tall inside me, a hankering so strong it's like pain, but there's no regret, no shame, no turning back.

"I don't want to blame you, Marshall," I cry.

"Ah, don't be so good all the time," he says softly.

And we go spinning down together, Marshall and I, to the place where memory dwells, untouched by real life, pure and good and white like a new peony bouncing on its careless stem.

"Come here," he whispers, pulling me beneath him. His skin is cool, he surrounds me like water. Beneath the surface of the world, we listen to our hearts beating as we sink. All our petty sins forgotten, erased, beaten smooth as shells at the bottom of the sea.

Seven

What about the girl, Ettie, on the Nile, sleeping off rum and bad dreams and a sorry little life? She exists, lies pasty flesh and bird bones on a plastic mattress in the bowels of this seedy motel. And Corinthia, in New Orleans, rising with her hangover to feed her sickly kid cereal and soda pop for breakfast. What a thing to wake to, imagining Marshall in the pale arms of these girls, making love, their thin legs like limbs of birch wrapped around his slender hips.

I hate your careless, selfish lust, Marshall. To be one among many is nothing to be proud of. Just another woman with a secret between her thighs. A secret anybody knows.

I want to stop thinking, lying down beside the length of Marshall on this sticky seat and closing my eyes, trying to make up a good dream. Be married to me, Marshall. Please just be married to *me*.

The sun, hazy and pale over the tar roof of the motel, finds its way into the car. I pick chigger bites on my ankles, smoke a cigarette as I wait for Marshall to wake. A dog wanders along the edge of the sleepy motel, picking through fallen trash around a dumpster. He gets a snow cone stuck on his long nose and can't get it off, thrashing against the gravel to knock it loose.

Marshall's done some bad things in his life, rumors like scraps of old letters with the last sentence missing the words that would reveal it all. Something about a knife, a scramble over a twenty-five-cent cup of beer and a girl's pale hair. And where did he get his money? Not always from playing the piano. He never asked me for money, but he always had some in his pockets, crumpled bills on the dresser at night, enough for whiskey and cigarettes and crawfish. Enough to buy himself a new jacket, a pair of boots, a bag of reefer. Enough.

Marshall turns in sleep. I hear his skin tear away from the hot vinyl seat. I watch his eyes open on the new day, wondering what day, what car, what girl.

"Hello, Alice."

That voice, like something promised, coins poured into an empty hand, a drink of water in the desert. Those brown arms reaching to pull all the girls in the world down upon him.

"Are we someplace nice, Alice?"

"We're at the International Motel. In the parking lot."

"Oh well," he says, and lifts the flask to his dry lips.

I wait for inspiration, a handful of words like winning poker cards that will turn him toward me, give me power over the future.

"What about the girl, Marshall?"

Wrong. I know it already. Always the wrong question on my lips. A pair of deuces instead of a flush. But why do I have be so careful all the time with Marshall?

Why do I have to plot conversations like war, worry over nuance, inflection, tone?

"What girl?"

"Ettie. In the motel room."

Another swig. Another minute. I wish I had no worries in the world. Tell me, Marshall, tell me I've got no worries in the world.

"What you want me to do bout that girl, Alice?"

I shrug, slowly raise unknowing hands to the sky.

"I got to get back to the rig today."

There it is, fear like a scurrying rat, building its nest with my hopes. He won't come home with me. He won't tell me I have no worries in the world.

"Why?"

"I'm due on the dock at noon."

"Why don't you quit?"

"I doan wanna quit."

The sun, too flat and hot; I want to push it away. I want to tear this skin off and run away into a different self.

"Miss Hilda died."

If I could laugh, I would. This must be the sorriest thing I've ever said. Marshall gazes at me, mystified.

"I ain't goin home now, Alice."

"By why? Why won't you?"

"I got to make some money first. I'll call you when I get to town."

What am I? Another girlfriend? One among many. How many calls will he make when he gets to town? How many girls will need to know that he's back, available, ready for anything?

"You got me confused, Marshall. I don't know what to do."

"Go home. Tell Mama I ain't dead."

"Marshall . . ."

He looks up, his lips pursed in suppressed irritation. Then suddenly, blankness like a shadow falls across his face and he smiles as innocently as the baby Jesus on a Christmas postcard. I can see myself in his pupils, how pitiful and ugly I've become. I look hard and try to find something about Marshall to despise so I can drive away with some dignity. But it's hard. He's so uncommon, his beauty so inexplicable I can't take it apart, can't find the hidden flaws.

I climb over the seat and get behind the wheel. I look at my hands in my lap, waiting for Marshall to get out of the car. He takes his time, stretching, lacing his workboots, raking his fingers through his hair.

"Get out, please."

"Goodbye, Alice."

He's standing over me. He reaches inside and touches my nose with a finger. This stupid gesture is the final indignity, something to placate a child. In this bright, bitter moment, I could run him down with the car and feel no remorse. Just drive away, into another future. Forget we ever met and did so many wrong-headed, reckless things to bring us to this moment.

Eight

The wind hurries shadows of clouds across the pale wood floor. Twenties rustle listlessly on the blue bedspread. Sixteen twenties. Ripe, newly plucked, an evil green like weeds on the side of the highway. I sweat just looking at them, my palms moist, my arms sticky against my ribs. I ought to give this money back to Boy; it seems unwise to be indebted to him, but I'm going to look at it awhile. These bills are so new! They even smell new; there's no whiff of palm dirt, wallet leather. Just a green, acrid scent like pickles in brine.

Rain weeps down the panes. The warm, restless wind gives the curtains a shudder. It's Penny's birthday today and I haven't gotten her a present. If I show up at her birthday party without a present, she'll be disappointed, or mad. I hurry into my clothes, slip a twenty in my pocket, and take the streetcar down to Canal Street to the Maison Blanche department store. At a cosmetics counter I buy her an atomizer, a delicate blue bottle shaped like a swan with a silky rubber globe to squeeze out the perfume.

On my way back to the streetcar, I veer down into the Quarter and stop at the Acme Oyster House. Percy is shucking oysters, his shiny brown hands moving rapidly, gracefully, popping the shells open one by one. He shucks five or six before he notices me.

"Did you read yore paper this mornin, Alice?" he says distractedly, packing big chunks of salt around the opened shells on a tin platter. The bar smells of gumbo and beer. Fat men with bibs around their necks hammer crab shells with butter knives.

"Did you see that article bout the mailman?"

"What mailman?"

"That Whistler guy, our mailman."

Another shucker in a big canvas apron is sitting two seats away, drinking a Coke and reading the paper.

"Gimme that paper, Horace," Percy says, whisking it from under his nose. He slaps it down in front of me.

I scan the front page. The government is building missiles. A sheriff in a parish outside of New Orleans wants to ban Negroes from the city streets during the Christmas holidays to keep crime down. A mailman has been arrested by the FBI for tampering with the mail. Mr. Henry Whistler of 2351 Tonti Street has been charged . . . the public may inquire about their mail at the Central Post Office beginning August 23. . . .

"Mr. Whistle?" I feel a twinge of guilt, commiseration, as though he were a relative. The mail's been screwy lately, mostly fliers and advertisements. But Mr. Whistle stealing the mail?

"Why would he do that?"

"Dintcha read it? They say he bin stealin money, old people's social security checks and stuff like that."

I imagine Mr. Whistle reading the mail, the personal letters, steaming them open from a kettle on a hotplate in some stuffy little midtown shotgun. Pretending to live in other people's lives. Maybe if you're a mailman, and you've got no friends or relatives and nobody to write you a letter, it's too terrible an irony to live with.

"You spect the FBI goan read our mail, Alice?"

"Why would they?"

"Cuz they nosey. That's what the FBI do, ya know. They go round bein nosey alla time, lookin in people's windas, tappin they phones . . ."

"You got something to hide?"

"No, mam. I'm clean. Ain't I, Horace?"

Horace looks up from the shiny surface of the bar, his face stoned with boredom. His skin is black as a plum and his bottom lip is delicately curved, a pale pink against the dark of his face. He opens his mouth to speak and his voice is deep, raggedy as a rusted saw.

"You," he laughs, pointing a finger at my breast, "you be too clean fer this world."

Boy calls to me from their screened porch, as I head home.

"C'mere, you got to hold this for me." He struggles with a long paper banner that says: HAPPY FORTIETH BIRTHDAY PENNY! I grab an end and follow him into the dining room.

"She's bin forty for the last five years," he grumbles, climbing onto the middle of the table to hang crepe streamers from the light fixture.

"Mama said to come over at seven." He tosses the paper roll at my head and lights a cigarette, catching the streamer on fire. The fire races along the colored paper until he reaches out and crumples the small flame in his fist.

"When you goan pay me back my money, Alice?"

"I thought you told me I could take my time."

"I'm a little hard up for cash. Ain't ya got fifty bucks you could throw my way?"

"The party's starting in half an hour. I'll go home and get changed and bring it back with me."

"Oh, all right. Jest don't let Mama see you give it to me."

I leave him on the dining room table where his tennis shoes are making dusty prints on the polished surface. Outside, it's too hot to breathe. I walk slowly, with my head down, and don't see Lucy Nell sitting on the front steps until I get to the middle of the yard. She storms down the walk to meet me, her balding suede pumps clacking on the pavement.

"Garden hose," she says. And that's all I need to know. She's come to take back a hose she lent us a year ago.

"In the garage, I think."

"You know he's in Morgan City," she says, following me around the side of the house.

"Yeah," I say, hoping to sound regretful.

"Yes, girlie, girl. He called me. What you gonna do bout it?"

I have to sit down on the cool cement steps to absorb this news. She folds her liver-spotted arms across her chest and glares at me. She looks like a goose. A long-necked, nasty goose.

"He said he'd come back when he got off the rig," I lie.

Lucy Nell snorts and waves her purse in my face.

"You went down there and you didn't bring him back?" she screeches. "Girl, that man left you!"

She turns away, disgusted, and stomps around the house to the garage. I follow her. Marshall's father ran off to Florida ten years ago with a checkout girl from the Winn-Dixie before he died of alcohol poisoning. I don't mention this to Lucy Nell. I don't point out the parallels in our situations.

"You shoulda called the manager," Lucy Nell says. "You shoulda explained the situation and brought Marshall home where he belongs."

Lucy Nell is always calling the manager. Managers in stores all over New Orleans shake in their boots when Lucy Nell walks in.

"They don't have a manager. They have a receptionist and she doesn't know much."

"If you really wanted that boy back, you'd find a way, little missy. Now, where's that garden hose? I ain't got time to listen to the mewlin of a girl what's got as little sense as you. You doan know how to keep yore husband home. You jest don't."

"He'll be back soon," I reassure her. "I expect to hear from him anytime now."

"I bet you money, you don't." She yanks on the heavy door. We get it halfway up and we both move toward the middle. She turns, her face close to mine, and I smell Sen-Sen, hair spray, a warm, oniony whiff of human steam. I'm desperate to get away from her, so I heave the door with all my might, pushing it skyward.

"I jest bet he don't call," she hisses. "I know him. He's my son."

Well, I'm his wife, I think, and you're probably right. He won't. But I never thought he'd call you either, and he did. That's one for the history books.

Lucy Nell goes into the dark garage and finds the hose hanging from a rusty nail on the wall.

"There's a hole here, Alice. Yore gonna have to buy me a new one."

I follow her back around the side of the house. She carries the hose in a large coil over her shoulder, like a man, and heaves it into the trunk of her car, grunting and puffing and sending me dirty looks.

"I never liked you much," she says. She slams the trunk shut and wipes her hands on her dress. I stare at her, wondering what to say, but my head is full of aimless air and I stand helplessly experiencing the sting of her last confession.

"Same to you!" I scream, watching her car turn the corner.

Boy is waiting for me beneath a tree in the front yard. He steps out of the shadows and scares me out of ten years of life.

"You got the money?"

"Don't do that. Don't sneak up on me."

I spy Mama Lapere in the front window, watching us like an old buzzard, her neck wrinkled like gray crepe.

"Here." I shove the money into his hand. "I coulda given it to you inside. I don't know why it's such a big secret."

"Mama'd start hittin me up for money alla time, that's why. You plan on stayin long?"

"Who wants to know?"

"I'm jest askin." His hair is tucked up under a black baseball cap and he looks exposed, pale, a little girlish.

"Aren't you coming in?"

"Yeah, yeah, I'm right behind ya."

Penny's in the kitchen, mashing potatoes with a blue plastic spoon. She's got her big purple chiffon dress on again and an apron with straps too short to reach around her waist. Her guests sit drinking beer around the kitchen table. Mama Lapere and two women in waitress uniforms and nametags that say: Welcome to Artie's, Home of the Soft Shell. Betty and Mary.

"Get Alice a beer," Penny tells Boy.

"Ain't Mayo sposed to come?" Betty says. Betty is skinny and flat-chested, and her mouth is rimmed with icy pink lipstick. She is at least sixty years old and she's wearing thick, flesh-colored support hose beneath her dingy white uniform.

"He said he'd come," Penny says, plopping spoonfuls of potatoes into a plastic serving bowl.

"Come sit here by me." Mary pats a flamingo chair and I sit beside her. "What's yore name, sweetie? Have you got a boyfriend?"

Mary is probably in her sixties too, her pale hair tinted a pinkish hue. Her uniform is so tight, the seams are split under the arms and I can see the stubble on her armpits when she raises her hands to shake down her dangly bracelets.

"Alice is married," Penny says. "But her husband's gone away."

"Is he away on bizness?" Mary wants to know.

"He run out on her. He's bin gone for months."

Penny shakes a spatula in the air, sprinkling melted butter on the floor.

"But yore so pretty!" Betty cries as though prettiness could prevent all manner of humiliations.

Mama Lapere blinks and snuffles into a wadded Kleenex. Sitting so close to her, I notice a humming noise coming from deep in her chest. She sucks beer from a long-necked bottle and the hum goes away.

"Why'd he run out on you, honey?" Mary leans in for an intimate account. Boy hops up on the counter and drums his heels against a cupboard below. He stares at me, smirking, eagerly scrubbing his bottom lip with the back of his hand.

"He's working on the rigs. I went to visit him this weekend. He's gonna come home soon." I don't know why this sounds like a lie.

"Ahh." Mary sighs knowingly. She's heard this one before.

Penny ushers everybody into the dining room and turns off the overhead lamp so she can light candles on the table. As the room goes dark, Betty trips over a rumple in the rag rug and falls against me, knocking me into a hutch filled with Elvis knickknacks. I watch, horrified, as an Elvis decanter wobbles and falls on top of an Elvis Christmas tree ornament, shattering it into little bits.

"My ornament!" Penny cries. She begins to weep. She covers her face with her hands, and there are mashed potatoes dried on her knuckles.

"I'm so sorry. I'll get you another one."

"You cain't," Penny sobs, "it was one of a kind."

"I seen them things all ova the place," Betty assures her. "I kin git you one tomorra."

"Oh, all right," Penny snaps. She stops blubbering immediately, and her face is clean of tears.

There's a place set for Mayo at the head of the table and Penny watches it mournfully throughout the meal. The only thing that seems to make her feel better is a discussion of Marshall's faults. She spends a moment or two describing Lucy Nell with great relish.

"White trash," she intones. "From Arkansas."

Betty and Mary listen with interest, arranging and separating the different foods on their plates, and Mama Lapere snores in her seat, her elbow resting in the bowl of a soup spoon. Boy eats voraciously, looking up now and then to wink at me. At one point, he can't get enough black-eyed peas on his fork so he scoops a pile onto his fingers and stuffs them in his mouth.

"Alice will remember this," Penny chatters. "One time Marshall stole Boy's old red wagon outa the garage and used it to barbecue chicken. He put some coals along the bottom and an oven rack over the top and grilled himself some chicken wings. Ruint that wagon, he did, and it had sentimental value to me. Boy's daddy bought him that wagon when he was five. I wanted to have that wagon forever, but now it's all black and burnt on the inside. Ain't none a my grandchildren ever gonna use it."

Mary shakes her head. Betty sighs and snuffs out a cigarette in her empty salad bowl. Boy laughs and steals Mama Lapere's T-bone off her plate.

"Then this one time I woke up in the middle of the night cause there was all this racket goin on outside. Dogs barkin and people shoutin, and I go downstairs and there's Marshall with a car full a dogs. They're all jumpin at the windas and carryin on, and I says to him, Marshall, what are you doin? And he says, Miz Lapere, they're paying two dollars a dog down at the animal shelter cause a them dog gangs roamin the streets, and I'm fixin to make me some money. Never worked a day in his life, that Marshall."

I don't remember either of these stories about Marshall. I have a vague recollection about the barbecued chicken, but I didn't know he'd gotten the wagon out of Penny's garage.

Boy stands up and he's got the tablecloth tucked into the top of his jeans. He starts walking away and the dinner plates slide across the table following him.

"Boy!" Betty screams, and grabs for a dish of peas. Boy's plate clatters to the floor, but it's empty and it doesn't break.

"Where you goin?"

"I got things to do." Boy yawns, stretches his arms above his head. The corners of his mouth are shiny with steak grease.

"Well, goodbye and good riddance," Penny hollers after him. "He cain't even say happy birthday to his mama," she complains when she hears the screen door slam. "He cain't even give his mama a present. If only every child could experience childbirth then maybe they wouldn't be so selfish."

"Amen," Betty says. "Why dontcha open yore presents now, Penelope?"

Penny smiles slyly and pushes her plate away to make room for her gifts. Mary stumbles into the kitchen and comes back with a big box wrapped in newspaper comic strips. Penny tears off the paper and rustles through the tissue inside to find the hidden presents: a coffee cup in the shape of big, pink pendulous breasts; a plastic blowup male doll, "Anatomically Correct," it says on the box; an airplane-sized bottle of Dry Sack sherry; and a tortoiseshell comb with a silver-plated handle which they found at the flea market in the Quarter, Betty explains. Penny passes the presents around. The comb is missing three teeth, and it feels oily as though it went straight from somebody's hair onto the sale table.

I push my present toward her and Penny rips at the paper greedily.

"Oh, Alice!" she whines, pulling the atomizer from its box. "I already got me one a these on my dressin table. Well, I hope you kept the receipt. I'll pick somethin else out tomorra."

I'm feeling a little forlorn by this time. I follow Betty and Mary into the living room for after-dinner drinks and sit down on the couch, trying to think of excuses so I can go home. Penny flips through record albums and Betty mixes martinis at the rolling bar.

"I'll tell you a secret to keep yore husband home," Mary whispers, settling herself on the couch beside me.

I look over at her, take in her pancake makeup, her shellfish smell, and her red plastic earrings shaped like little crabs.

"Do you want to know?"

"Sure." I nod vigorously as though this is the secret I've been waiting to hear all my life.

"Git you some a them long fake fingernails," she confides. "Men is crazy bout them fingernails, take it from me. You jest glue em on and they won't fall off less you do the dishes. Then you got an excuse not to do the dishes, too. Honey, take my advice, git you some a them fingernails, paint em a bright red or pink, and that man is yours for life."

We stare at one another for a moment. I don't know what to say. She fiddles with an earring, crunches ice from her highball glass.

"You kin get em at the K and B drugstore," she says, looking expectant.

"Thanks," I say. "I'll remember that."

When Penny puts on a Don Ho record and drapes a streamer across two chairs so we can limbo, I slip into the kitchen for a glass of water and then out the door until I reach the back steps of my own house. I take a beer from the refrigerator and walk through the foyer into the living room. At the picture window, I watch Mayo park his car in front of Penny's house. He's carrying a big box wrapped in silver metallic paper with a bright fuchsia bow. He stops at the gate to pat his hair in place with a licked palm.

"Jest put it in the corner over there, Lumey. Jesus, I got to tell you how to pick yore own nose!"

Boy's voice comes out of nowhere so clearly I think he might be outside in the front yard. I walk back into the foyer and start for the front door, but a sliver of light catches my eye from the top of the stairs. The trapdoor to the attic is halfway open. I wait for a moment, and a ray of light bounces through the opening and disappears again.

I hear Lumey's voice as I tiptoe up the stairs. "How come yore makin me do all the work?" he complains. I set my beer down on the floor and softly ease the attic steps down.

"What the hell are you doing, Boy? Where did all those boxes come from?"

Boy jerks up, peers at me from beneath his cap. His hands rest on the air above a cardboard box. He's trying to smile, but he's not sure there's anything to smile about yet. Lumey drops the flashlight and it rolls across the floor toward me until I can reach out and grab it. I shine the light on Boy's face.

"How come you ain't at Mama's birthday party?" He raises a hand to shield his eyes.

"That's not the question. What are you doing in my attic?"

Lumey inches over to the window and pretends to watch traffic go by outside. His big head looms in the dim light.

"I'm gonna move this stuff tomorra, Alice. I jest need to put it here for tonight."

"What is it?"

"Jest some stereos. A buddy a mine bought em . . . for his family . . . they're presents, ya know. He din't want to spoil the surprise."

"He's got a mighty big family." I count the boxes, fifteen or sixteen in all.

"He's Catholic, ya know. They got big families."

"You're fulla shit. You get this stuff outa here now. You stole it and you're keeping it here till you can fence it someplace."

"Alice, you bin watchin too much TV. I cain't move it now. I got to wait till tomorra. You owe me money, remember? I helpt you out when you needed it, so now you got to help me."

I hold the flashlight in his face and wait. We glare at each other, Boy and I, wondering what will happen next, who will give first. Lumey has found Cleva's okra and is twisting the lid off a jar.

"Okay. But if you don't get this stuff outa here by tomorrow, I'm calling the police. I mean it."

Boy looks at Lumey, his clumsy fingers stuck in the jar. He smiles. Lumey smiles back. Hapless, yet smug.

"Ain't she a nice girl, Lumey?" Boy says, scratching his skinny chest. "I tole you she wuz a nice girl."

I follow them down the attic stairs, and Lumey stumbles at the bottom, kicking my bottle of Dixie across the hall floor. Beer sprays along the walls, foams at his feet. He takes a bandana out of his back pocket and mops at it feebly.

"Just get outa here," I say.

When I hear the front door slam behind them, I notice I've still got their flashlight, and I follow its beam back up the attic steps. I sit in the yellow chair and shine the light across the sloping walls, wondering what Marshall was doing up here, leaving footprints on the dusty floor. Maybe he was doing the same thing Boy was doing. Maybe he was hiding from the doorbell, the phone, his mother, his buddies, himself. Or me. I get tired just thinking about it. I turn off the flashlight and listen to the awful silence, years of dust muting the world outside.

Nine

*E*arly the next morning, Percy stands by the car waiting for me, picking lint off his black bartender's jacket. We drive to the post office to pick up our mail. The parking lot is jammed with cars, and we have to stand in an endless line that trails all the way out into the parking lot. Percy looks nervously at all the people shuffling against him. A skinny woman with pointed catlike glasses carrying a plastic bouquet of flowers is jabbering in front of us. When she turns to glare, I see she's applied her lipstick above her lips, beestung. She stares me down until I have to giggle. Percy starts to laugh too, and we're soon bowled over, a little afraid of our mirth and all the people pressing around us.

Finally, Percy is at the front of the line and he tells the clerk his name. The clerk fishes a pile of mail from a wooden box and slaps it down on the counter in front of us. There's a letter from Percy's mother in Florida that looks like it's been crumpled, wadded up, and stuffed back into its envelope. Percy opens it sadly and smoothes it down on the counter as I wait for my mail. I'm not trying to look, but lines jump off the page, and I don't stop myself from reading. Somebody named Gerald is getting out of jail at the end of September. Percy's sister is having an operation, female trouble. Percy's mother wants to know when he's going to send money, when he's going to come home.

I tell the clerk my name and wait. There are three letters, a few bills, and a pile of junk mail. I turn, the bundle clutched against my chest, and look at the long line of people behind me, their faces fluttering, sharp and batlike.

When we get back into the car, I look at my mail. A letter from my mother, a letter from the Magruder Oil Company, and a warning from the electric company for nonpayment of services. I hold my mother's letter in my hand. Her stationery, the blue of a robin's egg, is so familiar yet forgotten, I want to cry.

I have a vision of my mother as I feel the crisp linen paper between my fingers. I assemble her features, clothe her like a paper doll, imagine her in sunglasses, her pale hair pulled back severely from her face, tall, leggy, elegant, and intimidating. We look so unlike each other except for our skin and pale hair no one would guess she's my mother.

I look down at the letter again, listen for her voice, try to measure the pointed silences between her words. She's still mad, hurt, disguising her discouragement with trivial anecdotes. She's smarter than me, smarter than Marshall and me together, too clever to betray her feelings over something she can't change.

She refers to Marshall as "your husband" and never utters his name. Has your husband gotten a job yet? she writes. Does your husband want to come home with you for Thanksgiving or Christmas?

When I try to imagine taking Marshall to Ohio, I get hives. It seems impossible, Marshall in Ohio, sitting in my mother's unlived-in living room, trudging through the snow to my grandfather's house for a holiday dinner. Marshall in a parka, Marshall's nose dripping in the cold. Marshall and me sleeping in my candy-cane room on those chaste, single beds, listening to the house settling, the radiator's hiss, my mother's insomniac puttering around the house.

I skim her letter, looking for confessions, revelations, condemnations, the fury she needs to unleash on me for my defection, my marriage to a stranger. But she's merely conversational. News of my father's latest ulcer cure, my grandfather's sick and dying dog, a description of a woman she works with who always wears a turban, a house she's trying to sell. The distance in her tone is much greater than the miles I've put between us, more devastating and ominous. Suddenly, I know I will never take my husband home to meet her.

"Whaddo you think this one from the oil company's about?" Percy looks over my shoulder at the mail on my lap. "Mebbe yore husband is writin you a letter."

I put my mother's letter aside and drive the car across the street to a Pack-a-Sack convenience store to get some cigarettes. When I get back to the car, I light one and look at the mail again.

"Open it, whydontcha?"

"What?"

"The letter from yore husband."

I'm curious about it, but the letter from my mother is stuck in my craw and I can't stop fretting over it. I pick up the Magruder envelope and exhale, trying to feel calmer.

Percy peers over my shoulder as I rip it open. It's a form letter:

> Dear Mrs. Bettonville:
> We have lost record of your ___husband's___ where-abouts since ___August 13, 1979___ . This could be due to a number of things which our office cannot be responsible for. Enclosed is a final earnings payment. Thank you for your patience.
>
> Sincerely,
>
> Bernard Lasko
> Executive Director

A form letter to report a missing person! Men must float in and out of that oil company's doors all the time, faceless and disloyal. There's no final earnings payment in the envelope, which means maybe Marshall didn't go back on the rigs after he took his vacation with Ettie at the International Motel. Maybe they went to Las Vegas after all.

"Lemme see," Percy says, and I hand him the letter.

"It doesn't mean anything," I say dully. "It means Marshall went to Las Vegas with some little slut, that's all. He was probably scheduled to work and he didn't show up. I'm sure it happens all the time. That's why they have a form letter."

"I think you should call em, Alice. Call em right now. Ask em why there's no check, too. You deserve a little money, dontcha? There's a pay phone right there. You should call now."

"I don't want to call. And I don't want Marshall's money. Anyway, maybe the mailman stole it."

"But you could pay back that loan to the guy next door. And if he's run off with this woman, then you got a right to the money, don't you?"

"Oh, all right. I'll call. Do you have change for the phone?"

A man with a long cast on his leg is sitting against the phone booth eating an ice cream drumstick. I step over him and get inside. Maybe I should call the number for time and dial-a-prayer instead. Percy would never know. But I don't lie very well. I look at the top of the letter and dial the number there.

"Mrs. Bettonville," the receptionist repeats nervously after me. There's something wrong. She tries to make me think she doesn't recognize my name, that I'm just another routine call, but there's something shrill about her voice saying my name. She transfers me almost immediately to Mr. Lasko.

"Oh, Mrs. Bettonville," Mr. Lasko says in a voice sodden with gravity. "I'm afraid . . ." he begins slowly.

What are you afraid of, Mr. Lasko? Tell me, give it to me so I can take it away from you. So *I* can be afraid.

"I'm afraid we've located your husband, Mrs. Bettonville," he drawls. "The body has been positively identified by other members of his crew and by a piece of identification found on his person."

"The body?" We must have a bad connection. His voice sounds very far away. Suddenly I feel sleepy. The littered, sticky floor of the phone booth seems to rise up to meet me. The man with the broken leg bangs his cast against the booth as he struggles to get up.

"Your husband is dead, Mrs. Bettonville. I'm very sorry."

"I'm very sorry," I parrot. I don't believe him for a moment. I saw Marshall only two weeks ago. "How?"

"He drowned," Mr. Lasko says, and his voice gathers a certain dignity as though drowning was the most noble of deaths, something to be proud of.

"I saw him, Mr. Lasko. I saw him a few weeks ago."

"Mrs. Bettonville," he says patiently. "We've been trying to locate you for a week now. Your husband's remains were cremated. I have an envelope here containing his personal effects. His mother, Mrs. Lucy Nell Bettonville, has been notified. She arranged for the cremation."

"When?"

"Two days ago. We had trouble locating her, too."

Why didn't she call me? Why didn't she come over to take the rest of Marshall back, his shoes, his deodorant, his T-shirts, and toothbrush. Why didn't she come to blame me?

Percy stands outside the booth, the tips of his shoes pressed against the bottom of the door. I stare at them, unable to look at his hopeful face.

"Mrs. Bettonville," Mr. Lasko continues, "if you could just come to our office in New Orleans when you're feeling better, we'll arrange for some kind of compensation."

This sounds so businesslike. People die every day, take their living selves lock, stock, and barrel and disappear. That's the truth of it. I put the phone back on the hook.

"He drowned, Percy."

"Yeah?" Percy says, as though he wouldn't expect

anything else. He folds a long arm around my shoulders, presses his cheek against my hair.

"Marshall is dead."

Percy just drives. Outside the city, the air is heavy with Queen Anne's lace, sweet william wilting on the sides of the road. A billboard advertises a snake farm where we can see a live boa constrictor eat something as large as a man. Thousands of yellow butterflies coast along the breeze, fluttering through the windows of the car.

I have to imagine at least once, the drowning. Marshall in the water at night, the sky a black curtain studded with cold, faraway stars, and Marshall, wet and startled, hollering, his voice puny over the noisy engine of the boat. Then he realizes it's no good, he won't be heard, and he smacks the water in anger with his fist, his legs churning and already tired. A sudden calm steadies him, he leans back against the waves to float, to look at the moon and the endless sky, to study his wrinkled fingers. After a while, he's just gone, down, down, his body no longer light and willing, but dumb as a bag of rocks.

"You kin cry, Alice," Percy says.

I can cry, that's something I know for sure. But Marshall could have done something to stop it. He knew how to swim. He could have held his breath, gone limp and easy along with the waves until they took him someplace where he could crawl from the water like a crab. But he let go, he didn't try, he did it on purpose. He just forgot there were people and things waiting for him, a life to finish—tired of it all, listless, bored with whiskey and

117

long nights and girls lined up waiting for him like ducks in a row. Tired of love and time and trying to be.

"Maybe he wanted to die."

Percy frowns, swerving from potholes, his eyes wide and far away with wonderment.

"Some people get tired of lookin at pretty things," he sighs. "They stare at the chickory on the side of the road, or the legs of a girl danglin out of a car winda, and they say to themselves, that ain't nothin. That ain't no help to me. That pretty thing ain't goan make me rich or satisfied; God doan live there in the sky, and no debil from hell is goan haul me screamin into the dark fire. And then, they got no choice, cause the sweets doan mean nothin no more. They go to the place what's left for them. The only place dey's any promise."

I watch his face, his lips moving. This is the most he's ever said to me, maybe the most anybody in the world has ever said to me. Comfort lights on my shoulder for a moment. For just a moment, until I hear Marshall's words: "I'm always doin somethin ugly, but it don't matter anymore . . ."

"What place, Percy? What's the place with promise?"

"Down in here," Percy says, placing a long, brown hand on his chest. "Down in here, where you is the only God."

Percy stops at the drugstore before he takes me home. He comes back to the car and takes a little box out of the sack in his hand.

"Sleepin pills," he says, offering them to me on his outstretched palm.

"I don't want them."

"It's always good to sleep," he insists.

When we get inside the house, he ushers me to the couch in the living room and takes two pills out of the box.

"I got to git to work, Alice. I'd feel better if you took the sleepin pills." He gives me a plaintive look, and I pick the pills off his palm and put them on my tongue. They're chalky and bitter, and once I hear the back door slam behind him, I spit them into my hand. I sit on the couch for a while, staring at a dead begonia in a small green ceramic pot on the coffee table. The front doorbell rings and I continue to sit, watching the begonia as if it might grow new buds and resurrect itself.

"Alice, ain't you gonna open the door? It's Penny."

After a moment, I hear the knob turn and she lets herself in.

"That black boy came by the house and tole me bout Marshall."

She's wearing a purple muumuu dotted with pink orchids, and the colors make my head ache. I'm still clutching the sleeping pills, damp and partly dissolved now in my tight fist. Penny sits down across from me in a brocade chair, arranging the folds of her muumuu over her chubby knees.

"Pore girl," she cries. "Mebbe you should git some sleep."

She watches me intently as though she fears I might take a knife from my pocket or tie a bedsheet around my neck and hang myself. I must be doing something wrong, my grief inappropriate. She seems to want something from me, a display, a few racking sobs as evidence. She raises a quizzical eyebrow, leans forward to pick up the box of sleeping pills.

"Pore girl," she says again, her breath ripe with bourbon.

She shakes the box of pills nervously and glances over at the TV set. She's inappropriate, too, I'm thinking. She doesn't know what to do and longs for the comfort of television life. After a moment, I get up and walk over to the TV. A soap opera blooms on the screen, a man and a woman in hospital garb, gesturing excitedly, showing each other charts. I go back to the couch and lie down. Penny and I watch, relieved we have something mindless to pay attention to. She takes a pint bottle of bourbon from the pocket of her muumuu and passes it to me. The room is quiet, the TV has no sound. We pass the bottle back and forth until it's done.

I will never see Marshall again. Not in a room, not on the street, not on this planet. Never be caught inside his eyes, smoothed down by his hands, quickened by the sound of his voice. If there was a point to his dying, a blessing, maybe I'd go along quietly, give up, give in, let go. But he's no symbol, no cause to fight for, just a boy who drowned, and it doesn't make any difference who he was or how hard he loved or how many people are waiting for him, longing for him, watching at windows for the sight of his face, because he's still dead. And after a while nobody will care, they'll forget him and the world will not even have stuttered or skipped a beat at the loss of him.

Penny's gone and I sit in front of the TV watching voiceless mouths open and shut, thinking about how all these people preserved on video tape are going to die and nobody is going to care that they won five hundred dollars on "Truth or Consequences." This is a rerun anyway; they're probably already dead. I crumple the brown begonia's dry leaves in my hands and wonder what I'm doing here in Violette's house with Violette's old magazines and her furniture and her knickknacks and linens and ghostly scarves. I don't belong. I have never belonged. Belong, be long. Marshall don't be long. Don't be long, someone come and say it's a mistake.

Memories unfurl like tails on runaway kites. I reel them in, bring them into focus, remember Marshall and me on our honeymoon in Pass Christian, Mississippi. Standing in the brackish water in my new two-piece bathing suit, the first two-piece I ever owned, while Marshall sifts sand through his brown fingers, watching the waves come and go. A shrimp boy walks by on the beach, the shiny shells of his catch flickering on his fingers.

The sky at dusk a lavender ribbon.

"Your new suit," Marshall whispers, proud as though he'd picked it out himself, his arms slipping against mine, the scent of his skin like sweet straw. I did love you, Marshall; I did love you. I couldn't help it.

In the evenings, we stand in the doorway of a cheap motel room along the Gulf Highway, watching teenagers in hopped-up cars roar by, tossing beer cans. Watching the evening tumble down like a silk slip through a pale woman's arms. We dance in a bar in Biloxi, listening to old black men playing trumpets and saxophones, our faces shining with sweat, our hands nervous with desire. Later, we walk down a long pier over the gulf and watch fisher-men in dinghies putter up to the dock, the floors of their boats glittering with fish scales. Inside the marina, Marshall buys me dried shrimp in a little clear package, an unbreakable comb. The chalky salt of the shrimp in my mouth. The plastic comb, unyielding.

Sometimes, when I lie down on the couch and close my eyes, I can hear Marshall talking inside my head, saying things I'd forgotten he said: "When you die, I bet you come back as a dog . . . God is dog backwards, right? As far as I kin tell, God just might wanna make dogs outa us all. . . ."

Marshall sleeping. Marshall's good teeth. Who will wear his clothes? Who will inhabit his space? If only I could take this sadness off like a coat and walk away.

Ten

*M*y bones are stiff as I rise from the couch to stretch and search the cupboards for something to eat. I stand at the sink, looking out into the yard and running cold water on my fingers for no good reason. A stray dog chews his tail in the gazebo. A white, puffy dog like the fluff of a dandelion. It's Marshall, I think, back from the dead as a dog, looking for a nice home. But it's not going to run over here and tell me the secret to everything.

Marshall should have a funeral, I suppose. Everybody has a funeral or a service of some kind. Maybe Lucy Nell has planned something. I take the car keys from the counter and walk outside to the car. It's evening, the sky is dark teal, and the Dog Star is rising. The dog perks up and scampers across the yard toward me, but his haste makes me skittish and I dart inside the car and shut the door. He comes along the side of the car and scratches at the door, but I don't pay any attention. I look at the peeling paint on the garage and start the engine. Whining, the dog is whining, it's enough to make me go mad. I slap at the door to make him get down, but he doesn't. I rest my elbows on the steering wheel and gather my thoughts before I confront Lucy Nell. I wonder what to ask her. How to phrase my questions so she won't get outraged like she does and do something outlandish. There must be a way to communicate with Lucy Nell, to get on her good side. But I can't think of anyone she likes. Anyone who's won her favor, besides Marshall.

The dog races the car down the driveway, yapping wildly, his tail waving behind him like a flag. When I get to the street, I peel away, showering him with gravel.

Lucy Nell's brother Ned is sitting on the front porch in a plastic chaise lounge with a paper sack between his enormous bony knees. He takes a sweet pea from the sack and examines it carefully before he slips it into his mouth. Ned is older than Lucy Nell and deaf. He has a dog, Spottie, a cranky, sway-backed mutt. Ned takes Spottie everywhere. There's a bed for Spottie on the front seat of Ned's truck. Once Ned even brought Spottie to Lucy Nell's church though he wasn't well received by the congregation.

I think Ned likes being deaf. He seems to take pleasure in oblivion. He doesn't lip-read or wear a hearing aid, and he always misinterprets what you've said.

"Hullo, Vicki," he says when I come up the walk. Ned always calls me Vicki; I don't know why. "Spottie," he drones softly into the shadows. "Come up and say hullo to Vicki."

"Hi, Ned. Is Lucy Nell home?"

"She ain't on the phone." Ned smiles. "Did ya bring Spottie a little treat?" At the mention of a treat, Spottie waddles out of the shadows and sets his thick butt on

Ned's foot, an expectant look on his pointy dog face. "Gowan," Ned coaxes. Spottie gets up and sniffs my tennis shoes suspiciously before he gives me a vicious nip on the ankle.

"What are you doin here?" Lucy Nell cries, appearing behind the screen door, her gray- and strawberry-colored hair electrified under the porch light. She's carrying a scrub brush and a bucket of dirty, soapy water. Pushing the door open, she sloshes water on Ned's boots, but he doesn't notice.

"I'd like to speak to you in private," I say.

"There ain't nothin you can say that Ned cain't hear."

"I'd like a beer, too," Ned says.

"He didn't want to be cremated," I say. This isn't what I wanted to say. I don't know if it's true.

Lucy Nell is weak around the gills from crying, her eyes rimmed in red. She looks twenty years older than she is. I feel sorry for her for a moment, until I see that look in her eye, blood and revenge. Lucy Nell on the warpath. I step back instinctively, knowing this is going to get nasty.

"You bin gallivantin with a nigger," she barks. "Didn't think you'd care much one way or ta other."

"You know that's not true," I whisper.

"Nellie, lookat this pea," Ned says, holding it out to her. It's a twin, two tiny balls grown together, siamese.

Lucy Nell slaps it out of his hand and starts to cry, dancing around the porch with the awkward lurch of a whooping crane, her long neck darting in and out. I try to maintain some composure.

"Will you have a memorial service? Do you have his ashes?"

"I ain't gonna tell you," Lucy Nell sobs.

"You have to tell me."

"There ain't gonna be no memorial service. His ashes remain with me."

"I think I should have the ashes. I was his wife."

She leans in close, her breath spicy, her crazy hair lit by the porch light like a halo around her clenched face.

"You bin chasin my boy down like he wuz sumthin that belonged to you . . . but ain't nobody owns my boy, ain't no woman kin have my boy." She begins in a whisper, her voice gradually rising a trellis of hysteria, her spittle on my cheeks.

"You get outa here now, Alice!" she shrieks, waking the birds in the trees, their high chatter scattering like marbles in the dark. She holds up the bucket like a threat.

"'I ain't lettin you have nothin!"

I inch backward, stumble down the steps, watching the water in the air, arcing, dirty tears caught in light and time, wasted. The water swoops down over me like a shroud, bringing darkness, a shadow over my heart.

At times, I forget why I'm crying, confused to be worthy of such prolonged heartache. My head is cold inside and out from the effort. My eyes sting, my mouth fills with a sour taste. It seems ironic to expend all this energy on something that can't be changed. Marshall isn't listening, he doesn't care that there's grieving going on. But it seems this is the only way to speak to the dead, or to Marshall, if he's really dead. And truly, I'm not certain that he is. I'm mourning just in case, which is sort of like believing in God just in case. But I don't really believe that he's dead. I felt him somewhere this morning, like a lost limb, an arm still tingling where it used to be.

Marshall is out there somewhere.

From the front porch where I've been sitting since dawn, I watch Mr. Hooter mow his lawn, the new mailman make his rounds, the stray dog eat Penny's sugar cookies off a plate on the porch swing.

Boy slams the front door and shambles down the walk, his shoulders hunched, his head tucked against his chest. I can tell he's drunk by his shuffle, the loose roll of his head when he stops to look around. At the gate, he stops and gazes across the dead grass at me.

"Alice," he says in a flat voice.

"Boy."

"It's goin to rain."

I look into the dishwater sky, nod in agreement. It's always going to rain somewhere and rain is no disappointment to me today. I feel flat as paper, washed out and hung to dry.

"You goan have a funeral for Marshall?" He cocks his head, peers beneath a hank of greasy hair.

"His mother's doing all that."

"I swear I seen him jest this morning, in Jackson Square. Carryin round this monkey puppet. Musta bin sumbody what looked like Marshall," Boy muses.

"Musta bin."

"I seen this guy today who din't believe that Marshall was dead. Marshall owed him money, see? Marshall owed a lotta people money." He coughs, wipes his mouth with the back of his hand. "But he's dead and he don't care."

This is news to me, Marshall owing money. But maybe that's why he wouldn't come back with me from Morgan City.

Boy shuffles across the lawn, trips drunkenly on a tuft of grass and stops at the bottom of the steps.

"You need a gun, Alice."

"What for?"

"I'd git me a gun if I wuz you. If I had everybody and their brother chasin me down for money, I'd git me a gun."

"I don't owe anybody money."

He chuckles, shakes his head, incredulous at this daffy, small-town patsy who thinks she won't be held accountable for Marshall's money troubles.

"Yore so—stupid sometimes. How come yore so stupid, Alice? Sometimes I think you ain't such a dumb broad, but then you jest . . ."

"I just what?"

"That Marshall had balls." He smiles, changing the subject. "He could out-scam the scammers. He always had his finger in a pie."

"What are you trying to tell me?"

Impatient, he glances about, raps his knuckles in a drumbeat on the porch railing.

"Marshall weren't no saint, Alice."

"I know that."

"No. No. I don't think you do." He sidles up the steps, pokes a finger in the air around my chest, bringing his point home.

"You think you wuz Marshall's only girl? Marshall had plenty girls. He had girls all over town."

"I know about Corinthia."

"Corinthia!" he whoops. "That chick with the skinny kid? I din't know bout Marshall and Corinthia. Sweet Jesus!"

His admiration makes me queasy, but I fall back on the numbness that's cushioned me like a cocoon for days.

"There's nothing you can tell me I don't know about," I say flatly.

"That's where yore wrong, baby. I kin tell you things to curl yore hair." He makes a drunken sweep with his arm, includes the world and all the sorry saps milling around in it.

"But there's sumthin troublin me, Alice. Sumthin maybe you kin splain since there's nothin you don't know about . . ."

I look past him, as though disinterested, steeling myself for whatever will come next.

"How come . . . how come a girl such as yoreself, a pretty girl, a nice pretty girl with a college education, how come a girl like you would put up with Marshall's shit?" He squats so we're face to face. "Look at the facts now. This fella was a Romeo. He had more girls than fingers. He run out on you and din't even drop a postcard to say goodbye. Tell me, why would a girl hang round for that? I want to know. What did Marshall have over all you women? Wuz he blackmailin you? Wuz he jest some kinda incredible stud? What's the answer here, Alice?"

Ernest Boy, his face screwed up with sincerity. He really wants to know. He believes there's a secret to learn, a formula, a magic incantation. I hold my elbows, close my eyes against his cruel, hopeful face.

"I loved him."

Boy snorts. For him, it's not enough. And even to

me, it sounds pompous, a little pathetic. What good has it done me? It's brought no dignity to my small life. And I begin to wonder why any woman would stay with a man like Marshall. Corinthia and Ettie and me and all the girls I don't know about, powerless before Marshall's unerring gaze, pliable and obliging as dough. But maybe Corinthia and the others lead reckless lives too, and for them, Marshall was just one among many. Perhaps I was the only constant, righteous and naive, playing house by myself, slow to realize that rules are negotiable, or made to be broken. Even in death he has made me feel unworthy of love, and it galls me that I have let him get away unscathed.

Boy looks up into the darkening sky, watches steely blue clouds scud across the tops of the trees. Something begins to uncoil in my chest, a taut spring whizzing loose, and I'm terrified, panicked. Like a mechanical doll, the key in my back twisted a notch too far, my own undoing.

"I bin thinkin bout the money you owe me, Alice."

"What money?"

"The thousand I give you. I could use yore attic for a while and then you won't have to pay me back. We kin call it free and clear. What was wrong with yore car anyway?"

"It needed a new transmission. It cost six hundred dollars."

"Jesus, Alice! A transmission don't cost six hundred dollars, even brand new. You wuz robbed. How'd you git this far in life lettin everybody an their brother take you for a ride?"

"Oh, shut up. How was I supposed to know? The mechanic said six hundred dollars and I gave him six hundred dollars."

"So, what about it?"

"What?"

"The attic, the money."

I consider this for a minute.

"No. No, I don't think so. I'll just pay you back as soon as I can."

I'll get another job, start going to the bingo games at the church down the street. I don't ever want to see Boy again. I don't want him in my house or my yard or even living next door.

"No. Yore sayin no?"

He swallows, licks his lips, watching my face. I look away. I don't want to think about the money and the car and Boy's boxes anymore. I don't think this should be part of my life, my cross to bear.

He leans down, his face so close to mine I'm cross-eyed looking at him and I have to jerk back to stare at his drunken face, his wild curls, his anger emanating from him like a purple fog.

"You ain't got no sense of humor," Marshall once told me. "For you, everythin's a matter a life and death." I knew he was right. But now I feel like laughing out loud, looking at Boy, his skinny weasel face, his arms akimbo on his shapeless hips.

"You goan be sorry," he hisses.

I reach out, touch his sleeve.

"I'm already sorry. I can't get much sorrier than this."

His hand darts out and clutches a hank of hair at the nape of my neck. He jerks me to him, my face almost pressed against his chest. Laughter burbles from my lips; I can't help myself.

"This isn't the way he did it." I look him square in the eye, my voice cruel and controlled. "Marshall never got a woman like this . . ."

Someplace in a bar, I don't notice its name. On every corner there's a bar, always open. A bottle with your name on it beneath the smoky mirror where you can watch your shadowed face, pretend to be a stranger. The floors are sticky with spilled beer; the air smells of grease and garlic, cut with the sickly odor of disinfectants sloshed around in toilets. I slip off my stool after a few shots, my mouth dry with too much alcohol, but my tongue is finally loose, the knot of tension in my shoulder blades dissolved.

It's late evening when I saunter home, grateful for alcohol, for forgetfulness, grateful for God's wisdom and small pleasures. The wind whips around the corners of the house, moaning like a harmonica. A hot wind, full of rain, playing havoc as it sweeps through the windows, tossing curtains, scattering papers, knocking back cupboard doors, as insidious as a poltergeist.

The sky falls silver blue then lightens to an eerie yellow, casting an unearthly light, the couch more blue, my T-shirt a living green. Oranges in a bowl on the table seem to pulse. I'm nervous, drunk, a little jittery. I look out the front window, watching for the money lenders coming to get me, coming to sell my house and clothes, Violette's furniture, coming to get back what's theirs from Marshall.

The rain begins as I go upstairs to bed, falling hard and noisy as though the roof was tin. In the bathroom, the wind fills the shower curtain and it billows over the tub.

There's a black, greasy ring of dirt in the tub, gray fingerprints on its porcelain flank. I kneel to look at them, and I can see the lines and whorls on the prints, as personal and individual as a voice, a signature. I place my own fingers over the smudges to see if they fit, but the prints are bigger, longer, not from a woman's hand. I wonder whose fingers they could be. Somebody dirty, somebody who's just put down a fresh newspaper. Somebody who's been inside my house and taken a bath.

I peek into my room: the unmade bed, clothes balled up on the seat of the wicker chair, a wet towel on the floor. I touch the towel, smell it, hold it close to my face. Somebody's here. I scan the room, looking for some protection, but all I can find is an old parasol of Violette's in the closet. Nobody walks around with parasols anymore, it seems a stupid thing to own. Maybe I could poke somebody to death with the pointed end of it, just in case.

I take the parasol with me into the guest room. The windows closed, the room empty and too tidy. I whip open the closet door, jump back, and raise the parasol. Nobody there, just hatboxes on the shelf, a pair of men's slippers on the floor. Something's missing, though. The suit. That old-fashioned pearl gray suit with vest and cuffed pants that Violette kept for my grandfather's visits.

I hurry back into my bedroom and pull the phone into the closet with me. I dial Percy's number and listen to it ring six or seven times before a man picks it up. "Percy, you want Percy?" he croaks. He drops the phone and I can hear his bare feet slapping on the linoleum floor as he makes his way down the hall to Percy's room.

* * *

"This is nutty," Percy complains as he follows me up the stairs. He pushes past me into the bathroom and studies the ring.

"It's like tar," he says, drawing a finger through it. "Goan take some elbow grease."

"And the suit . . . Violette had a suit hanging in the closet in the guest room. It's gone."

The guest room is cold, mute, wearing the indifferent expression of a motel room. Percy sits on the bed, his hands hanging between his knees. He chomps a piece of gum, cracking bubbles.

"Should I call the police?"

"They jest goan laugh at you."

"Maybe you could stay over tonight?"

"I kin sleep right here," he says, patting the guest bed.

Wind rushes through the hallway downstairs, sending the dining room chandelier into a twitter of tinkling crystal. Heat lightning pulses against the sky, filling the room with its eerie light.

"Yore like flypaper, Alice," Percy says softly, snapping his pink gum. "Trouble always stickin to you."

Eleven

*T*he mailman brings the mail early, slopping through puddles along the sidewalk, muttering to himself. He's older than Mr. Whistle, with faded red hair and a face the color of putty. He stuffs a big manila envelope into my box.

I rush out to see what it is, once he's gone. From the Magruder Oil Company. I rip through the envelope and dump its contents on the kitchen table. Marshall's wallet, a thin slab of soft black leather like a piece of burnt meat. Marshall's St. Christopher medal. Nothing else. I open the wallet. Driver's license, expired, with a picture of Marshall that makes him look like a convict. A library card. That's a laugh, Marshall in a library. A folded scrap of paper with a phone number. A local one, and I guess whose it is.

I pick up the phone in the kitchen and watch the plastic rotary dial spin.

"Hello," a woman answers, her voice breathy and tired. My head fills with a whirl of thoughts. I'm about to say something ugly.

"Who's this?"

"Who's this?" she chirps back. I hang up. I look her

name up in the phone book. The number's the same. Corinthia Jones, Cajun chanteuse, husband thief, vamp in a red dress. It doesn't matter anymore.

Touching Marshall's wallet, I feel something, a hum beneath my fingertips. I stroke the soft leather, the stiff edges, trace my finger along white watermarks where salt from the gulf has dried. You must be dead, Marshall. These are your things.

Percy emerges from the attic, four or five jars of Cleva's okra in his arms.

"How come you got all them TV's and stereos up there, Alice?"

"What TV's and stereos?"

No use pretending, Boy's been back. I don't understand the mechanics behind his little scams, but the police will be here some day, waiting for me, accusing me when I tell them about Boy.

"Never mind, Percy. They're Boy's."

But I get an idea. An idea as bright as the glitter of coins found between the seats of a car when you're desperate for money. A small idea, but big enough to do the job. Percy and I go up into the attic again. We bring the heavy boxes down one by one and drag them into the front hall. Thirteen boxes in all. Four stereos, seven small color TV's, and two bandbox radios. All a little used, but not damaged. We cart them into the front yard and line them along the walk where they can be seen by God and everybody.

Penny's in her yard in her bathrobe, picking up empty beer cans and a bag of soggy potato chips, split open and strewn across the grass.

"Damn kids," she groans, stooping to snatch a can under a bush. "Never have kids, Alice. They ain't nothin but heartache."

"Is Boy home?"

"He's upstairs, sleepin. You kin go up if you want." She almost falls off her high-heeled slippers bending to grab a handful of wet chips.

"What's in them boxes on yore lawn, Alice?"

I stomp past her, up the steps, through the door, and into the front hall. Boy's not in bed. He's lying on the couch in the living room, drinking beer and watching a soap opera with the volume turned up to a nearly deafening level.

"How come you ain't at work," he says, not bothering to look away from the TV. He's wearing an old plaid robe and a pair of black socks with holes in the toes.

"I got a vacation."

"I spose you want sumthin from me, Alice. Or maybe you've bin thinkin bout my offer." He takes a swallow of beer, looks at me over the top of the can. His hair lies flat as though he's been wearing a stocking cap, the curls matted down and damp with sweat.

"I found that stuff you left in my attic again. The stuff you stole. I'm gonna call the police."

"You owe me," he says, looking at the TV.

"You better come get it or you won't like what happens."

He puts his feet on the floor and studies a jagged toenail that's broken through the end of the sock.

"I got you a gun." He reaches inside his robe pocket and brings it out. A small, snub-nosed gun, dull black and evil looking. For a moment, I think I've made a mistake, bringing Boy's loot into the front yard. I think I've underestimated him, forgotten what he's capable of. He points the gun at me, but I won't take it.

"I got all your boxes out on the front lawn waiting for you."

He looks up slowly—it seems to take him hours to look at me with those big empty eyes, the sense gone from them like a light snuffed out. He walks to the door, passes his mother without speaking.

"What's with him?" Penny cries, standing in the doorway with her trashbag full of wet chips and beer cans.

He stands at the hedge staring at the boxes. In the bright light of the sun, he looks pale like something that lives inside, dead white, a boneless, grubby thing.

"Don't try an outsmart me, Alice."

I feel faint for a moment. A fly dithers around my face looking for a place to light. As I swat it away, my anger returns, a noisy rattle in my head, growing louder as I wait beside him.

"You get your stuff. Stay out of my house," I whisper.

"I got to tell you sumthin, Alice." He stares at the boxes on the lawn as though they might grow legs and walk away.

"What?"

"I seen Marshall."

"Marshall's dead."

"No, he ain't." He turns to face me, and though he's not taller than me, he seems to be looking down from a great height.

"You're nuts."

"Take them boxes back inside and I'll tell you where you kin find him."

His face is sober with honesty, as if he's telling the truth, almost noble now in his bathrobe and damp socks. But I can't believe this truth, and no longer want to.

"Will you take them boxes back if I tell you?"

"You're crazy."

"Why don't you go see?" he asks slyly. "Why don't you jest see fore yoreself?"

Twelve

I doan think you should go," Percy says. "Sounds fishy to me. One day he's dead, the next day he ain't. The oil company sent you his things. Where'd they git them things if he ain't dead?"

The Acme Oyster House is crowded and hot. Percy works furiously cracking oyster shells while he talks, never looking up from his work.

"Well, I'm gonna go see. It's just around the corner on Esplanade and Rampart. I want to be sure."

"Thas not jest around the corner," he says. "Why doan you wait till I kin go with you?"

"This is something I should do by myself, don't you think?"

"What if it's a trick? What if this boy is robbin yore house or sumthin worse while he's got you runnin all ova town lookin fer a dead guy?"

"I'm gonna go see, then I'll know. Maybe I'll stop back on my way home and let you know what happened."

"You better do that, Alice. You better let me know. I'm goan be worryin bout you."

* * *

The house Boy described is on the corner of Rampart and Esplanade. I sit in the car a few minutes, smoking a cigarette, watching clothes tumble in the dryers in the Laundromat across the street.

It's a tall, pale yellow house next to a vacant lot. There's a wrought iron fence and a narrow brick path leading to the door. In the evening light, it still looks grand and elegant if you ignore the beer cans in the small, overgrown yard, the dead azalea bushes beneath the front windows. There's a gingerbread dome on the roof, a widow's walk on the third floor, a wraparound balcony on the second, Victorian latticework along the eaves and windows, trellises choked with morning glories. But when you get close, it becomes a tenement, the paint peeling, the wood rotted, the gray pall of car and truck exhaust dimming its features.

I wish Percy was here. My mouth is parched, my lips sting when I lick them out of nervousness. I squash my cigarette in the ashtray and look at my face in the rearview mirror. How do I look? Does it matter? No, I'm expecting a stranger, not Marshall at all.

I get out of the car and shut the door softly as though afraid of waking a sleeping neighbor. I keep my eye on the long black windows of the house, expecting Marshall's face to appear. The foyer is dark, and the door shuts behind me. It seems airless in here. I can't get any breath, and feel as though a heavy hand is pressing against my throat, choking me.

Two doors to choose from. I hold a lit match up to a business card taped across the spyglass: MADAME VUARNET, CONSULTATIONS IN THE OCCULT, PALM READING, COMPETITIVE PRICES.

The floor creaks above my head and I listen to the footsteps receding down the hall toward the back of the house. The match burns my fingertips and I toss it to the floor. I step back outside and take a big gulp of air. The streetlamps blink on like magic and moths suddenly appear. Marshall's dead, for Christ's sake. And if he's not, he's gone from me anyway. I watch the bus unload on the corner of Rampart, old black ladies in thin cotton dresses carrying bags of groceries, big black pocketbooks slapping heavily against their thighs. I stand completely still, breathing in and out, in and out.

Two teenage boys, shirtless and lithe, their heads shaved and smooth, amble down the sidewalk. They stop when they see me and stand staring, their eyes hidden behind dark, mirrored sunglasses. Menace, inside and out. I'd better choose. I slip back inside and press my back against the door to keep it closed. The door opposite Madame Vuarnet's creaks open by itself. I can see up the stairs now, the walls on either side splattered with bright paint. What if I change my mind? What if the sight of Marshall makes me want him all over again?

Up the steps, I don't hear anything until I get to the landing. The soft static behind a radio voice, a clatter of silverware. Familiar sounds. I smell the mustiness of mildewed plaster, wet wood, the sharp, sweetish odor of roach killer. Somewhere, in another house, a telephone rings over and over again.

I pass three rooms down the long hallway, each empty of anything but walls, a floor, windows. Their vacancy is threatening, unforgiving. I shouldn't be here.

I peer into the last room at the end of the corridor. A man sits on the balcony outside the kitchen, his chair tipped back, his long legs resting on the railing. He spears something from a jar with a plastic fork.

When he hears the floor groan, he looks up expectantly toward the dark kitchen. There's barely any daylight left, but I can see him, wearing a suit coat and pants, pearl gray, old-fashioned, my grandfather's suit. Marshall. He chews noiselessly, squinting at me. I come closer, stub my toe on a three-legged chair, the only piece of furniture in an otherwise empty room. I step onto the balcony. Whole boards are missing from the floor and I can see down into the weedy rubble of a courtyard below.

"What are you doin here?" he says.

The moon is rising, bright, and clear, illuminating the empty lot so I can see the milkweed and jimson, the chickory's blue-headed flowers. A full moon, bloated and complacent, about to spill its milk into the night.

He follows my gaze.

"There was a dead body there yesterday." He points with his fork. "I called it in from the pay phone at the gas station. I stood here for the longest time, staring at it, till I realized it was dead. A big guy, his legs folded up over his head like a lawn chair."

"Speaking of dead people . . ." I stop. I don't mean to be flip. I don't want to lighten this moment. I can hardly bear the sound of his voice, but I force myself to look at him, to see who he really is, what he really looks like.

He coughs, his head down between his knees. His hair is faded and dull, his skin a grayish mustard color. He plucks an olive from the jar. I'm amazed at how unfamiliar he looks, or how unfamiliar I feel. Have you become the enemy, Marshall? Does all my sorrow begin and end with you?

"Everybody thinks you're dead. Your mother's got your ashes in a little jar."

"I heard bout that." He bites an olive in half, sucks out the pimento. "Boy Lapere told me. You remember Boy?"

I dare myself to look into his eyes, to see something remembered there, but they're dark, the pupils large and listless.

"I seen him yesterday," he adds. "He loaned me some money."

"Seems like a lot of people have loaned you money."

"It's true," he says, rooting around in the jar for another olive. "That's why I had to git outa town for a while. Ya know, Alice, this mixup bout me bein dead is just the thing. A dead man cain't pay back what he owes."

"Works out real nice for you."

For a long time, we're silent, watching the night spread to the edges of the vacant lot. There's no traffic on Esplanade or Rampart, which makes me uneasy. I need to know that life is going on outside as usual: cars gassing up at the station on the corner, drunks weaving out of Nietzsche's on Rampart, police cruising the neighborhood, maids walking home from the bus stop.

I feel hollow, gutted like a fish, glassy-eyed from looking at Marshall too long. How I hate to make these big mistakes, like Marshall once told me. I hate to be so irrevocably wrong, and somewhere I've gone wrong, very wrong, to have ended up here, in this horrible, seedy house with this strange man who's supposed to be my husband pouring olive juice through the rotting floor. I've begged, borrowed, and stolen to keep him and I don't know who he is, why I'm here, or even where I'll be once I come out on the other side. And Marshall just sits there, in somebody else's coat and pants, with evil in his hands, holding it out to me, pressing it upon me, saying *this is all that's left to us, this is what is real about the world.* . . . I have no power over this, my heart crumples beneath its sinister weight. I'm not certain even God can smash it. I hate him, and hate myself for giving up everything to love him.

"What do you want?" Marshall says, breaking the silence.

"Why aren't you dead? I wish—"

"You wish I was dead? Why don't you say it? It'll make you feel better. I'm at the end a the line here, Alice. An I ain't goin nowhere. See this place? I live here. I've always bin comin here and I jest didn't know it till this minute. Seein you, Alice, that's what's done it. Seein you shiver here, how you cain't touch nothin for fear it'll make you dirty."

"You didn't have to come here. You could have done something to stop it. It didn't have to be this way."

"You jest don't git it, do ya? Yore a smart girl, but sometimes you jest don't git it. You don't change what you are like you change yore shirt or yore shoes . . ."

He rouses himself, stands slowly and leans against the railing, his back to the lot.

"Blue moon," he says, tilting his head back and looking up at the sky. "Second full moon this month makes a blue moon. It's a rare thing. A sight to see."

He touches his forehead as though remembering something. I see bats coasting along the wind over the lot, gray clouds laced with the moon's silver light.

"Some fella on the rig was talkin up how he was goan

rub my nose in his shit, how he was goan git me fixed for all the money I owe people back here. He knew some a them people, see? He was goan make it bad for me—"

He stops the rush of words and presses his fingers against his brow again.

"You wuz a big mistake for me," he says softly, shaking his head. "I don't know what the hell I was thinkin about. . . ."

He tears the suitcoat off as though it's burning his skin and flings it on the chair. I stare at him, unmoved.

"This fella, he stole my wallet." He looks up at me as though he knows I'll understand, absolve him for his crimes.

"He took my St. Christopher medal. He tried to git my boots, but they fit so good, sometimes I don't take em off to sleep. . . ."

"Whose ashes does your mother have?" I ask.

"I had to hit him," he says, ignoring me, shrugging, his shoulders bony beneath the rumpled dress shirt.

"I heard sumthin crack in his neck, his head jerked back, and he fell. I never hit a guy so good, so true; my hand didn't even hurt."

"Who's dead, Marshall?" My voice is a whisper, but he looks at me as though I've shrieked. He raises his hands to fend off my words. I don't want to know who's dead, but this question must be asked. It's like a house on fire that I can't stop looking at, can't turn myself away from, no matter how gruesome the spectacle.

"That girl was there. Ettie," he says, seizing upon her name. "She'll tell you how it happened. Quarters and pennies rolled out of his pockets when I hit him, and she picked them up. . . ." His voice peters out, and he scratches his chin, thinking. "I don't remember what happened next."

I turn away. I think I can see where the dead body lay, a tamped down spot in the tall weeds in the lot. For some resaon, I think of the fur muff Violette gave me when I was eight, a dress of my mother's long forgotten, a dress I always wanted her to wear, peacock blue with mother-of-pearl buttons.

Marshall's hand closes on my wrist, damp and demanding.

"He got up then," he says softly. "I know he got up. Ettie could tell ya. But mebbe he fell in the water. Mebbe he wasn't steady on his feet and fell off the dock. That's what happened—it musta bin that way."

I look down at his hand on my wrist and jerk away from him in disgust.

Violette reappears, her face, her hands in long white gloves. A silly, vain woman with her Japanese fans, her baubles, her jewelry box like a child's coffin, her wide, coquettish blue eyes. Bribing me with candy and gifts for my full attention, my undivided devotion. I hate even her at this moment. See, Marshall, you've changed me quite a bit even if I haven't made a dent in you, haven't made a mark on your surface, or opened your eyes to anything new about the world. But me, I'm different all over. Even the sound of my name in your mouth means something new, something sorry and finished.

"Ahh," Marshall sighs and takes a long drink from the flask in his back pocket. He pokes it under my nose. I take it from him, bitterly, and sip.

"We got to get quit of each other, Marshall."

He hovers, his breath humming a desperate song, his cold lips near my ear.

"Don't," I wail.

For a moment, he looks as though he might cry, and I feel anger swell, like skin too small around me cracking, molting, a locust's brittle husk. I can't wait till it's done, can't wait to be shed of him.

"I got to tell you somethin," he says, trying to touch me again, trying to press his hand where my heart beats. His voice so urgent, pleading as though if he doesn't get to tell me, he'll go mad or die or run screaming into the night. I push his hand away.

"No."

"You gonna leave me, Alice? You got one good thought left for me, dontcha, Alice? I don't want you goin away mad. You kin remember one good thing, cain't ya? You won't always feel this way . . ."

"One good thing?" I wonder, my voice querulous and strangely gruff.

Incredulous, I back away, running down the balcony steps, falling through a cracked rung and clinging to the railing. I feel foolish for a moment, and relieved to feel something normal, I begin to laugh. Leaning over the railing, my hair in my eyes, doubled over in uneasy mirth. I can't stop, can't laugh any harder without crying, and I skitter down the rest of the rotten steps.

"Where you goin?" he hollers. He waits for no reply, then lobs the empty olive jar at my heels.

* * *

The dried-out weeds snap beneath my shoes as I wade through the lot. Too slow, I'm thinking. I pick up my feet, my knees rise to my chest as I lope above the goldenrod, the chickory. I soon get my stride and urge myself on. I watch the trees bowing, the stars mount the sky. I'm moving so quickly, the city blurs by me, cars, people, lights, sharp colors of night. I'm moving so fast, I soar above tar roofs, skim across treetops, hurried, yet finally calm. I have someplace to go and I can't take you with me. I have something to do and you can't do it too. I'm getting away. I'm leaving. And I don't have the burden of pity in my heart.

About the Author

SALLY SAVIC is a graduate of Tulane University and the Iowa Writers Workshop, and a recipient of two grants from the Ohio Arts Council. She lives in Columbus, Ohio.